Sexton Blake's Xmas Truce

By G. H. Teed

Illustrated by Eric Parker

Special Christmas Number - Complete
First published in the Union Jack magazine,
New Series, No. 1105, 13 Dec. 1924.

Stillwoods Edition

Stillwoods.Blogspot.Ca

Catalogue Information:
Title: Sexton Blake's Xmas Truce
Author: G. H. Teed (1881-1938)
Illustrator: Eric Parker
First published anonymously in the Union Jack magazine, New Series, No. 1105, 13 Dec. 1924.
This Edition by: Stillwoods, 2022
ISBN Canada: 978-1-989788-92-9
Blog: Stillwoods.Blogspot.Ca
Author Blog: http://ghteed.blogspot.com/
Storefront: http://www.lulu.com/spotlight/lulubook22

Special Christmas Number - Complete

A story of Sexton Blake, Mademoiselle Yvonne, and Huxton Rymer. Here you have a yarn with a real Christmas appeal--clever in treatment, novel in theme, and altogether seasonable. This absorbing account of the great detective's Yuletide Truce is going a long way towards giving you a Happy Christmas.

Other content: The Mystery of the Marshes by H. W. Twyman; Detective Magazine Supplement.

https://tinyurl.com/ve25d42s This link should go to a spreadsheet of all known Teed stories. The list is annotated with various information on the stories and my progress with recapturing the work.
The library of Teed's stories increases almost weekly. Check at the Lulu.Com for the latest arrivals. Search for Teed.../drf

Keywords: Sexton Blake, British fictional detective, Union Jack magazine

Cautionary Note: This series of books by Stillwoods are intended to make the stories of G. H. Teed, born in New Brunswick, Canada, available to collectors and researchers. The editor, or rather digitizer has not altered the original publication.

This story may contain language and racial terms that are not appropriate to today. I apologize for them; I know that the author was using his voice to excite and entertain an adventurous English audience. These works were published from 82 to 110 years ago. Most every work has characters of redeeming ethnicity within.

I hope you enjoy and share these stories; I have.
Doug Frizzle

No. 1,106. The PAPER with the DISTINCTIVE COVERS—The UNION JACK 5

SEXTON BLAKE'S XMAS TRUCE

A story of Sexton Blake, Mademoiselle Yvonne, and Huxton Rymer. Here you have a yarn with a real Christmas appeal—clever in treatment, novel in theme, and altogether seasonable. This absorbing account of the great detective's Yuletide Truce is going a long way towards giving you a Happy Christmas.

Some of the latest publications from **Stillwoods**.

The Pirated Cargo
The Grey Domino
The Sweater's Punishment
The Great Cigarette Mystery
Black Sea Sailor –Leonid Solovyev
The Beggar in the Harem –Solovyev
The Enchanted Prince –Solovyev
The Green Portfolio
A Soldier and a Man
The Affair if the Rotten Rails
Sexton Blake's Xmas Truce
The Affair of the Missing Financier
The Chocolate King Mystery
At the Turn of the Hour
The Sunken Schooner
The Black Emperor
The Idol's Spell
Dead Man's Rock –Q
The Adventure of the Giant Bean
Rosalie –Frank Parker Day
Victory Garden –Day
John Paul's Rock –Day

"ELEVEN more days, and I suppose something is sure to turn up to spoil things."

Tinker voiced the grumble as he whipped a date showing the figure 13 off the calendar block on his desk; and, as he heard the lad's voice, Sexton Blake half-turned in his chair.

"What is it, my lad?" he asked absently.

"I was saying that it is just another eleven days to Christmas, guv'nor, and that our plans were sure to be spoiled, as they were last year. It's a mystery to me why we can't get a free run over the holidays like everyone else."

Blake, who had been engaged on some rather boring detail work and was not averse to a brief break, lit a cigarette and swung his chair round. Then he regarded the lad humorously.

"What would you suggest then?" he asked.

"Chuck the whole blessed business and clear out," replied Tinker promptly. "Close up the show, shunt Mrs. Bardell off to her niece, and stick a notice on the front door saying we won't be back until after the first of January. That is my suggestion, guv'nor. And just to make sure, we could put on advertisement in the newspapers like a lot of people do when they go away, saying that letters will not be forwarded. On top of that we could change our names and go to some place in the country where we could get a bit of riding. I'm all for the peace and goodwill stuff this year."

"So it would seem, my lad. Unfortunately, in our profession, we are in the same position as medical men and—the police. Our holidays cannot be taken at any old time like those of the general public. But in spite of that I am rather inclined to agree with what you say. After our Christmas experience last year I should not at all mind a quiet day or two for a change.

"I don't think we could go quite so far as to placard the front door or to put a notice in the papers. That, in my opinion, would be just like an open invitation to several gentry of the underworld to get busy. As a matter of fact, I have been thinking something of the same thing, and have been wondering just what we might do. It has been a particularly trying year and I am tired—tired in more ways than one. We shall talk things over during the week and see what we can manage."

"There goes the bell, and that is just as likely as anything to spoil things," said Tinker, as the whir of the electric gong came from the outer hall. "I'll answer it, guv'nor— Mrs. Bardell's out."

Blake nodded and, jumping up, Tinker left the consulting-room. Blake could hear him as he went down the hall, then came the sound of voices as the lad conversed with someone at the front door. Following that, the door slammed and the listening Blake could detect the sound of double footsteps coming along towards the consulting-room, then the door opened and John Graves, Mademoiselle Yvonne's uncle, entered.

He shook hands with Blake, and, slipping off his fur-lined coat, sank into the chair by Blake's desk, stretching his legs out in the direction of the cheerful open fire. He accepted one of Blake's cigars, then, when it was well alight, he said:

"Been sent round by Yvonne, brought an invitation for you and Tinker, hope you will be able to accept. Want you both to come down to my place at Winfield for the Christmas holidays—Yvonne is having a small house party."

"That is most kind of you and Mademoiselle Yvonne," answered Blake with a glance towards Tinker. "I am sure nothing would please us better if we can manage to get away. It is rather a coincidence, but we were discussing the question of Christmas holidays just before you came in. At least, Tinker was doing most of the talking. He has evolved some very definite ideas this year."

Graves regarded the lad with a smile.

"What are the ideas, Tinker?"

"I was just saying to the guv'nor that for once we ought to shut up shop and clear out where we couldn't run into trouble. You have turned up in the nick of time, Mr. Graves. I hope you will get the guv'nor to accept. I'd like nothing better than to go down to Winfield, but I don't want as strenuous a time as the last was. What do you say, guv'nor? Can't we fix it up now?"

"As I remarked before, my lad, we are, unfortunately, not our own masters. I also should like nothing better than to accept Mr. Graves' invitation; but it all depends on how things are at the time. If our friends of the criminal world would give us a respite, then we could go without anxiety."

"Why not fix it so they will?" put in Graves. "Fix up a truce with some of them. Even the most inveterate enemies find a truce jointly beneficial at times. Or, better still, invite some of them along, too, so that you can keep an eye on them. It would be rather a unique situation to have such a mixture under the same roof."

"I've got an idea!" broke in Tinker excitedly. "Listen, guv'nor! Why not fix on a certain number to invite, as Mr. Graves suggests? We know Huxton Rymer, for one, is in England at present, and it wouldn't take us long to get in touch with him. Then there would be some of the others—if we could find them. You and Mr. Graves could fix on some other names of persons—a regular mixture. That would be a lot more fun than just making up a regular list—that is, if Mademoiselle Yvonne consented."

Both Blake and Graves seemed to feel something of the lad's enthusiasm, for the detective glanced at Graves, and they both laughed.

"Tinker is trying to get us into something as irresponsible as he himself would indulge in," said Graves. "But, at any rate, Yvonne wouldn't object. It would be fun, if it could be worked."

"How many could you handle?" asked Blake.

"Well, we already have a small list, but I could put up another dozen or so without any trouble. You know, Winfield is a very roomy old place, and more so than ever since I built on the new wing."

Suddenly Blake jumped up and strode across to the card-index cabinet. He drew out one of the drawers of this at random, and, recrossing the room, laid it on his desk.

"Now then, get a hat, Tinker," he said briskly. "Yes—Mr. Graves won't mind if you use his. Now then, I shall pick out a bundle of cards at random, just as I chose the drawer. Here you are." And as he spoke Blake took out some of the cards and dropped them in the hat.

"Now then," he proceeded, "Just for fun we shall ask Mr. Graves to draw, say, twenty of the cards. Then we shall see what happens. Will you draw, Graves?"

Graves bent forward, and as Tinker held the hat towards him he thrust his hand in and felt about until he had caught a card in his fingers. He drew this out, and laid it on Blake's desk, face down. Then he took another, and another, and so on, until Blake had ticked off twenty in all. That done, Blake swept the rest of the cards out of the hat, and dropped them back into the drawer for Tinker to arrange later.

Then he seated himself at the desk, and while the others watched attentively began to turn over and read out the names from the cards which Graves had drawn. About half-way through he paused over one of the slips of pasteboard and laughed before reading aloud the name.

"That wasn't one bad hit of yours, my lad," he said, "for here is a card bearing the name of Dr. Huxton Rymer. And here right under it is the name of Hermann Klein. You remember him, Graves, I fancy?"

"I certainly do," responded Graves grimly. "I am not likely to forget the man who was responsible for trying to poison Princess Molly, my starter for the Winfield Handicap a couple of years ago. If it hadn't been for you and Tinker, he would have succeeded in doing so. But he's still in prison, isn't he?"

Blake turned to Tinker.

"When would Klein's time be up, my lad?"

Tinker Jumped up and walked to the big bookcase where the red bound volumes of the famous "Index" were kept. He took down one of these, and after turning a few pages came to the record he sought. While he did so Blake and Graves desisted from the other occupation and watched him. Presently the lad looked up, and his lips moved silently as he went through a brief calculation. Then he turned to Blake:

"Why, sir, Klein must have come out about six weeks ago, allowing for the slice off for good conduct, if he got the benefit of that."

"Which he would, if I know anything about him," remarked Blake. "Well, at any rate, we don't want anyone of that kidney in the party." And so saying he took up the card bearing the name of Hermann Klein and dropped it among the others in the drawer. Then he resumed reading out the names, and when he had finished he looked up with an odd smile.

"Quite an interesting list, taken at random," he said. "There are some highly respectable people among them, and some first-grade crooks and sharpers, not to mention the small fry. What do you think of it, Graves?"

"I think a dozen or so chosen from that lot would make a highly choice mixture," answered Graves. "The question is, how to fix on the right lot. How could you get track of those we might choose?"

"Some we couldn't," said Blake. "That is why I selected twenty cards. And then, of course, we should have to reckon on several already being booked up for that date. But we could work on the list and see what happened."

"Then you mean that you would join in on this—that you and Tinker will come down to Winfield?"

"We shall accept, in any case. As for this other matter, I should like, first, to hear what Yvonne says. But I don't mind saying that I shouldn't at all mind having some of these gentry under a truce over the holidays, and it would certainly add a spice of interest to have them directly under my eye, besides avoiding any chance of trouble—and work."

"If they stuck to the truce," put in Tinker.

"Quite so, my lad—and I think they would. But what about putting up such a conglomeration at Winfield, Graves? What do you think Yvonne would have to say to the idea?"

"If I know Yvonne, she would fall in with the idea quite readily. She has been wondering in what way she could arrange something novel. I'll wager she would take up the idea, and elaborate it, if anything."

"Where is she now?"

"At the flat at Queen Anne's Gate."

"Then I suggest that we all drive round there and talk it over with her. If she agrees, I shall take it upon myself to get in touch with the persons we select; but if the crowd is mixed, I think it would be wiser not to let your highly respectable guests know the real identity of the others. If they got to know, your Christmas party would be in danger of developing into a case of nerves."

Graves laughed.

"I shouldn't worry much, with you under the same roof," he drawled. "And, anyway, that would add a little to the spice of the affair. There are two or three friends of mine from the club who are coming down. It would do me a lot of good to see them stirred up."

"Well, they might be at that," admitted Blake, as he rose.

Ten minutes later all three were in the Grey Panther on their way to Queen Anne's Gate, where they found Mademoiselle Yvonne in the smoking-room.

That charming young woman laughed softly when she heard the plan which had been proposed, and her eyes were roguish as she studied Sexton Blake, for it was rarely indeed that anyone found that austere person indulging in what was to be on the face of it, something quite out of his usual connection with crooks.

But perhaps it was the Christmas atmosphere already abroad; or, again, it may have had something to do with the fact that over the holidays she and Blake would be under the same roof together.

At any rate, Blake's interest did not abate as they discussed the pros and cons of the affair (and there were many to be considered when such a pot pourri was in prospect). It was left to Blake to get in direct touch with most of the people on the list, although Yvonne took it upon herself to send invitations to some of them. The list was longer than the actual number desired in order to allow for refusals on the part of those who had already made their plans for Christmas, and it was left at that for the time being. But it is safe to say that the little quartette of conspirators would have regarded it in a different light if they had guessed for a single moment what complications were to arise as the result of the unusual scheme that had been evolved by the trio at Baker Street—and by the spirit of Christmas.

As Huxton Rymer entered the place he almost stopped in his surprise, for Hermann Klein was seated talking to another man. And it was the sight of that other man—whom the world believed to be dead—that made him pause as if he were seeing a ghost. (*Chapter 3.*)

A FEW days after the events just recorded two men sat in the comfortably appointed library at Abbey Towers, a small, but extremely well-equipped estate not far from Horsham, in Sussex.

One was the owner of the estate, known in the district as Professor Andrew Butterfield, a gentleman of high scientific attainments, who was reputed among his scientific colleagues to be engaged on some particularly abstruse research work, and whose occasional contributions to the scientific journals were eagerly read.

In Sexton Blake's Case "Index" at Baker Street the same gentleman was better known as Dr. Huxton Rymer. But in certain circles of the underworld he was simply known as the "Doc," and his advice regarding the commission of crime (as was Sexton Blake's advice as to its detection) was eagerly sought, and paid for at a price that would have satisfied even the most fashionable Harley Street specialist.

His companion was a person of very different stamp. His clothes were shabby in the extreme; his hair and beard were straggly and unkempt. His face was bloated and of a purplish hue, showing the marks of many weeks' dissipation, and his eyes wore that sullen look which marks any man as "dangerous." And yet that same individual was not only still a young man, but, until six weeks or so before, he had been for nearly two years in a place where the regularity of toil and diet usually keeps a man in excellent physical condition, if not in content of mind.

That place was one of his Majesty's prisons.

Huxton Rymer had not been any too pleased when his man had announced the visitor.

"There is a man at the door, sir, who gives his name as Klein," he had said. "He has arrived in a hired trap from Horsham, and says you will see him when you know his name. He is, if I may say so, sir, a very shabby sort of person."

"There is only one Klein whom I can recollect," was Rymer's answer. "I was not aware that he was—er—in the country. Find out if his name is Hermann Klein. If so, I will see him."

The man had returned to say that the name was the one his master had suggested, and Rymer instructed him to show the visitor in.

"If Miss Trent should ask for me," he added, "say to her that I am engaged, but will be free presently."

(The Miss Trent to whom Rymer referred was Mary Trent, his secretary, who had once been at Abbey Towers as a housemaid, but who soon found out the secret of Rymer's livelihood, and had lost no time in proving to him that she could be of far more value to him as partner. But a deeper bond than that had soon sprung up between them, and now it was rarely indeed that Rymer moved without either the advice or the active participation of Mary Trent.)

It was not surprising that Rymer was a little puzzled over the name which his man had brought him.

Two years or so before he had given one Hermann Klein the benefit of his advice, and had, indeed, given him some active assistance in a scheme which had for its aim the undoing of Mademoiselle Yvonne and her uncle, John Graves. Those who have read the record which is marked in the Baker Street "Index" as "The Case of the Winfield Handicap,"[1] will readily recall the affair in which Sexton Blake disclosed the plot and enabled the police to lay their hands on Hermann Klein while in the very act of carrying out his swindle.

He had lost track of the time Klein had been in prison, but even while his man was talking he had made a rapid, mental calculation, and had figured out that it might well be the Hermann Klein whom he had known in the not very distant past. Rymer was by no means fastidious in his choice of male companions. More than once in the past he had found himself in a condition as destitute as that which his visitor presented.

Lately he had been more cautious with what money he had been able to lay his hands on; but none knew better than he that at any moment the turn of the wheel might see him stripped to the hide, and for that reason he was not indisposed just then to hold out a helping hand to Klein, even though he knew that Klein must know that he— Rymer—had tried to double-cross him in the affair of two years before, and would have succeeded in doing so had it not been for Sexton Blake.

Therefore, while his nostrils quivered with distaste at the spectacle which Klein now presented, and particularly so as he caught the whiff of spirits, of which the man's breath reeked, he was ready

---

[1] (See Union Jack No. 980.-Editor.) *available as a Stillwoods reproduction…/drf*

enough to shake hands, and before the servant departed told him to bring in glasses and a syphon.

"Well, my friend," said Rymer, when Klein had helped himself to a stiff peg of whisky-and-soda, "it seems obvious that you are not as prosperous as might be, and I am very sorry if that is the case. But perhaps it is a disguise? In either case, you have, apparently, come to seek my advice, so what can I do for you?"

Hermann Klein finished the last of his drink at a gulp, and pushed the glass unsteadily on the table.

"It's no disguise," he said thickly. "You seem to've forgotten what happened to me. D'you forget that I've been in stir?"

Rymer shook his head.

"Not at all, Klein. I remember that unfortunate affair two years or so ago. That was bad luck for you, and I can't imagine to this day how it came about. Can you tell me?"

"It was that devil Sexton Blake!" said Klein, with a sudden access of vicious temper. "You must know that much. If you had come to the races that day with me, as I wanted you to, it might not have happened. Didn't you get into any trouble over that business?"

Rymer gazed for a moment at the smoke which was rising lazily from his cigar. When Klein had first come in he had not known just how much the other guessed of his own part in that old affair, or if he suspected that he had been deliberately double-crossing him. But his first question had been sufficient to show him that Klein did not dream just how cunningly he had wriggled out of the whole thing, and he had not the slightest intention that he should guess now, after all the months that had passed.

Besides, it was now perfectly plain that Klein was "up against it" as hard as he possibly could be, and needed assistance. It all depended on what assistance whether Rymer's answer would be "Yes" or "No."

"Why, yes, there was some difficulty," admitted Rymer, after the pause. "But, you see, I had arranged for a quick getaway from England, if necessary, and I just managed to do it. I tried to get through to you both by telephone and by private messenger, but I was too late. I did not suspect for a single moment that Sexton Blake was on that job. If I had I should have advised you differently. But it is the luck of the game. So now, just what is it? If it is a case of monetary assistance—well, I am not very flush myself at the moment but I can manage something. Is that what you wish?"

Klein reached for the decanter without invitation, and deliberately helped himself to another stiff peg. The other drink had steadied his nerves for the moment, and he was beginning to get back some of the old sang froid that had distinguished him as a successful Stock Exchange operator in the City before the crash which had reduced him to beggary, and at the same time had put the stamp of the prison upon him. He scarcely diluted the spirit, which he drained quickly. Then he fixed his bloodshot eyes on Rymer.

"Money—yes, money!" he said, in the cold, icy tones that the spirit had steadied. "Money—you can lend me some. Look at me! Look at me! Hermann Klein—two years ago worth more than half a million, and now with nothing but the rags of what they gave me at the prison when I came out! Money—yes, a little. That is one thing I want. And that I will repay, for it won't be long before I have plenty again.

"But it is not the money which has brought me here to-day. I have come to ask you to help me in another way. And I have not come begging empty-handed— I have something to offer in return. I have no money just now, but I can tell you something which will be worth a hundred thousand pounds to you. When I first sought your advice two years ago I was told that you were infallible. I am not complaining about your part in that affair.

"But during the time I have been inside I have had time to think. To think, man! Do you know what that means? To think for hours, and days, and weeks in a cell where there isn't enough room to turn twice?

"You don't, but I do, and in that time all the ideas I had before have crystallised. And that is why I have come here to see you. I should have come before, but it was impossible. But what has brought me now is the same thing which brought me here two years ago.

"That smooth crook, John Graves, and that sly, man-eating devil known as Mademoiselle Yvonne, are rich and free and rolling in all that should be mine. Do you think I shall ever forget that they swindled my father out of Walla-Walla Estate, in Australia? Do you think I shall ever forget that it was that pair who ruined me, and put me behind stone walls? I want vengeance on them to-day as I have never wanted it before, and I have come to you, Dr. Huxton Rymer, to help me."

"You seem to forget that your father swindled them first in

Australia, and that it was you who let yourself in for what you got when you started on the warpath against them," murmured Rymer.

"I'm not forgetting that—I'm not forgetting anything! You are the one man who can help me in this business. I have not been idle since I have come out of prison. I have been busy gathering information about them. And I have a definite plan. But I need your assistance. Will you help me?"

"That all depends. Perhaps it would be better if you told me just what you have discovered, and what is in your mind. But bear in mind, please, that at the present time my slate is clean with the British police, and I shall take no part in anything which is going to alter that condition of things, unless—unless the prize is worth while. No—take my advice, and don't take another drink now. Wait until you have told me what is in your mind. But just a moment—the phone. I shall see what is wanted."

Huxton Rymer rose and went over to the telephone, which was ringing to announce a summons big with fate for both of them, could they have known.

HERMANN KLEIN sat moodily wrapt in his own thoughts while Rymer spoke over the telephone.

He paid no attention to what the latter was saying, but had he done so he would have seen Rymer give him a curious glance from time to time. Whatever the conversation was, it seemed to cause Rymer some amusement. He was smiling when he hung up the receiver and turned to his shabby guest.

"That is curious," he said, picking a cigar from a box and lighting it.

"What is?" asked Klein dully.

"Can you guess from whom that message was?"

"No. How should I?"

"Quite right. But it may interest you to know that it was from one of the very persons of whom you have been speaking. It was from Sexton Blake."

"Sexton Blake! Are you on friendly terms with him? It seems I have come to the wrong place for assistance!"

"As a matter of fact, I am not on friendly terms with Blake," said Rymer coolly. "And this is the first time I have had any communication with him for a long time. The message was not direct, but it was from him, nevertheless. And it may interest you more to know that Blake wishes to see me. The person who spoke on the telephone is a certain person up in London, through whom Blake evidently thought he could reach me. That is all I know, so far. But one never knows—it is possible this very fact may enable me to be of some assistance to you."

"You mean you will go to see him?"

"Of course. I shall lose no time in doing so. I am curious—distinctly curious—to know what he can have to say to me."

"What about a trap?"

"If you had listened to what I said you would have heard me ask that same question. I am assured that Blake is not laying a trap, and whatever my personal feelings may be towards him, his word is good enough for me. If he guarantees safe conduct, then he will keep to it."

"But what can he want of you?"

"How can I tell? I shall know soon, for I propose motoring through to London today."

"Then what about me? Can't you do something? I tell you I am completely destitute. As you see me now, so I am— utterly without other clothes than these rags, and not a penny to my name. I used my last money to pay the cost of a trap to bring me out here from Horsham."

"I shall do what I can for your immediate needs," said Rymer, with a glance of commiseration at the wretch. "But you will not get very far at the rate you are going. If you will permit me to say so, you look as if you had been soaking spirits ever since you came out of prison. That's no good to you. Apart from its immediate effect upon your physique and nerves, it only inflames your mind and clouds your judgment. If you propose embarking upon a campaign against Sexton Blake or the other persons you have mentioned, then you will need every ounce of caution you can muster. They are not to be tackled in any haphazard fashion."

"I can stop the spirits," said Klein sullenly. "There was nothing else to do. I had no way to turn. I only knew a day or two ago that you were in England. I heard it in a certain place in London, and I came on to see you as soon as I could."

"Well, I have said I will do what I can for your immediate needs. Whether I shall do anything to assist you in your campaign against John Graves and his niece remains to be seen. That will depend on what sort of a scheme can be figured out, and the only one that will interest me is one offering a substantial financial return. But I shall take you up to London with me, and give you, say, a hundred pounds with which to equip yourself. That is your most urgent need. After that—well, as I have said, we shall see."

Klein had no option but to place himself in Rymer's hands, and, to do Rymer justice, he intended giving the ex-financier a leg-up, even if he did not join with him in the scheme he proposed.

Hermann Klein, ex-convict and penniless, was a very different person from the opulent financier who had come to Abbey Towers two years before, and Rymer had no time or inclination to waste on those who were not going to be of some material use to him. As a matter of fact, his own coffers were getting low at the time, and he was on the look-out for something which would replenish them.

Klein did not seem to offer much prospect, but, on the other hand, he had hinted at having something in mind, and, since he had been no mean financier in the past, it was just possible that he might be able to advance some scheme that would be worth taking up. At any rate, Rymer would keep him in tow until he settled that point.

So after a private confab with Mary Trent, during which he told her that Blake had sent word that he wished to see him, he got out the big touring car and bundled Klein into it. He motored straight through to London, avoiding Horsham on the way, and as he came into Town drew up near a big well-known shopping emporium in Oxford Street.

Before leaving Abbey Towers he had given Klein a roll of notes, and now he said:

"You can get everything you need in that store. Go there now and have yourself completely outfitted. When you have done so, and have got yourself groomed up, go along to the American bar at the Venetia Hotel. I can't say how long I shall be, but the chances are I shall be there before you. If not, wait until I come. Then we will discuss matters further. I can't say anything until I know what it is that Sexton Blake has to say."

With that he drove round the corner into Orchard Street, and so into Baker Street, where he drew up in front of Sexton Blake's house. He mounted the steps boldly, and pressed the bell-button. Mrs. Bardell, Blake's housekeeper, opened to the summons, but if she recollected Rymer she gave no sign. He inquired for Blake, giving the name of Professor Butterfield, and she led him along to the waiting-room while she went to inform her employer.

Needless to say, Rymer was on his guard, and did not relax it on entering the consulting-room, despite the signs of holly and mistletoe and the genial manner of Blake, who was seated in one of the low saddle-bag chairs before the cheerful open fire.

Tinker was at his desk, and shot a look at Rymer as he entered, but beyond that gave the visitor no greeting. The lad was remembering the last occasion on which they had met. And now that the spur-of-the- moment plans which had been suggested by Graves' visit were materialising, he was not quite so keen to "mix it" with some of the proposed guests.

Blake, however, was looking forward to the affair in a whimsical fashion, and with as keen zest as ever. He smiled pleasantly enough while he waved Rymer to the chair opposite him. Then, when he had pushed a box of cigars across the low tabourette which stood between them, he said:

"Your visit, professor, shows that you received my message. I had not looked for you quite so soon. Apparently, our mutual friend had no difficulty in locating you?"

"None at all," replied Rymer. "And I came on at once. I am naturally a little curious to know why you wished to see me."

"I thought you might be. I shall tell you. As a matter of fact, my desire to see you arose through a suggestion made by my young assistant, Tinker. It was inspired, I suppose, by the general feeling which one usually experiences at this time of the year. It is something in the way of an experiment, and it remains to be seen whether it will be a successful one or not.

"The other day we were discussing things in general, and gradually the conversation worked round to plans for the Christmas holiday season. Christmas is now only a few days away, and with the assistance of Mr. John Graves, who happened to call in at the time, we have hit on a plan which I thought might interest you, among others.

"To begin with, Mademoiselle Yvonne, whom you have met several times in the past, had sent her uncle to invite me and Tinker to join them for a Christmas house-party at Winfield Grange, which, I imagine, you have no difficulty in remembering.

"My acceptance of the invitation depended on several things, which it is not necessary to explain. But it was then that a certain suggestion was made. Following this, I took from the drawer of my card-index file a bundle of cards, and these were put into a hat. Twenty were drawn, and each name written down. I need not say that at such a haphazard draw the result was decidedly interesting.

"Well—er—professor, among those names was yours, and I took steps to get in touch with you. I should have done so sooner, but for some difficulty in getting hold of the man who could tell me where you could be found. The exact item I have to pass on to you is an invitation to join this house-party. But, as I have already explained, it is dependent upon several things, the chief being a condition."

Whatever Rymer may have felt at this somewhat startling attitude of Blake's, he gave no sign beyond a smile. It was a decidedly novel situation to exist between him and the great detective, and while he was still on guard lest some sort of trap should be in the making for him, the proposal appealed strongly to his own sporting instincts, and up to the present he was half-inclined to accept. But he wanted to know more first.

"Just what is that condition?" he asked.

"A truce," answered Blake succinctly. "I think you must see that a truce would be necessary. By that I mean that for an agreed period of time I should have your word that in no way, by deed either direct or indirect, you would abuse the hospitality of the house where you would be a guest. I do not think I need speak more plainly than that."

"I understand you." remarked Rymer. "You seek a promise on my part, but what about you? Or about others in whose power it might lie to make things—er—embarrassing for me?"

"I should, of course, extend the same immunity to you that I have promised for the time of our interview to-day. And I should answer for others. I have said that the house-party would consist of a mixed company. By that I mean not only the persons who were selected haphazard from the bundle of cards which I picked out of the card-index here, but the personal friends who have been invited by John Graves and Mademoiselle Yvonne. There is, under such conditions, bound to be a good deal of opportunity for what I can only term undesirable violation of confidence, but I am prepared to accept your word if you give it in the unequivocal terms which I have named."

"And if I should give it and then break it?"

"That needs no answer. You are fully aware of what I should do."

"It would be more interesting, in my opinion, if we put the thing on that basis," murmured Rymer. Then, after a brief pause: "I am not disinclined to take you on your offer, but unfortunately, there is one difficulty in the way of my acceptance. You are aware that I have a secretary— Miss Trent. I had half-arranged Christmas plans for her as well as myself, and, of course, I cannot leave her alone over the holidays."

"I had already considered that." said Blake. "I am authorised, on behalf of Mademoiselle Yvonne, to extend the invitation to Miss Trent as well as to you—on the same condition."

Rymer tossed the end of his cigar into the fire and laughed.

"You are a sportsman," he said. "And the proposal appeals to me. Subject to Miss Trent's approval, I accept with thanks. As you say, I have perfect recollection of Winfield Grange, and I hope my stay there will turn out to be of a more agreeable nature than the last time.

"It remains to be seen after Christmas whether either of us has cause for regret. Yes, Sexton Blake, I shall accept—on that understanding; and if I do not keep the truce, I shall at least promise you that I shall give you fair warning that I intend breaking it."

"I shall take my chances of that," responded Blake grimly. "I want you to understand that while at first I was rather carried away by Tinker's enthusiasm over this affair, and John Graves' quick endorsement of it, I have not been so sure the last few days that it was altogether wise. At the same time, I have recalled that I have some cause to be indebted to you for the part you played in Hong Kong some time ago when Tinker fell into the hands of the Heaven-Born, and what you did then assisted materially in his rescue.[2]

"Don't think I did not, and do not, realise that you helped me for purely selfish purposes of your own. But we shall leave that aside. Play the game on this proposition, Rymer, and if you do you will find that I shall stick to my part of the bargain. Under those conditions we may both find this Christmas a pleasant change from that of last year."

Rymer rose and held out his hand, which Blake took.

"Agreed," he said. "I shall see what Miss Trent has to say about it, and will let you know by medium of the telephone. Ur—I suppose it would be out of order to ask what other persons will be there?"

"I am afraid I cannot answer that. You must wait until you get there. That is another condition of Mademoiselle Yvonne's. She wishes none to know exactly what others will be in the party."

"All right. I shall phone some time this evening and give you a definite answer." With that Rymer nodded to Tinker, and a moment later took his departure. When he was gone Blake looked at the lad and smiled.

"Well, that is another one booked, my lad it is going to be difficult to see just what your proposal is going to lead to."

"I think he will stick to the bargain, guv'nor," said the lad seriously. "His words sounded genuine enough."

"Um! That remains to be seen, my lad. There is going to be a good deal of wealth displayed by some of Mademoiselle Yvonne's guests, and I fancy we shall see some very valuable jewels at dinner, and in the evening while we are there. We know what Rymer is. There is no more predatory creature alive than he, and were it not that he has a clean slate, so to speak, at Scotland Yard, it would have been out of the question to give a moment's consideration to this proposal.

---

2 The full story of Sexton Blake's adventure in connection with the "Heaven-Born" will be given in an imminent issue.—EDITOR.

"He may intend now to keep the pact, but when he finds a heap of glittering wealth before his eyes, and realises that as a guest in the same house it might prove a comparatively easy matter to steal some of it—well, that temptation may be too much for him. I hope not. At this season of the year it would be very gratifying to have all that sort of thing swept away. I don't credit myself with any very forgiving nature, and certainly no criminal has ever given us more trouble than Dr. Huxton Rymer; but, after all, the man was once a highly respectable and respected member of Society.

"No finer surgeon ever wielded the knife than he, and—who knows?—some such opportunity to mix on equal terms again with those among whom he was once honoured may re-kindle the man's conscience—if he has one. At any rate, as a psychological test it will be interesting, and much good may come of it. Whether Rymer is incorrigible or not remains to be seen.

"And by the same token, while we shall take it for granted that he will respect the pact, we shall not be entirely unprepared for emergencies. If anything went wrong it would be a serious thing for Yvonne. Most of her guests don't know that some of the others are not exactly—er—Sunday-school teachers. Yvonne does know, and if anything did happen she would be held responsible.

"Also, we must not forget that she is still believed by some to be a ruthless adventuress, and it would be difficult to make the victims believe that she had not had some hand in any thefts that occurred. There are many ways in which we must regard this affair, Tinker. I reproach myself that I did not do so more carefully when you first made the suggestion. But we shall be prepared; we shall be prepared, both for our own sakes and that of Mademoiselle Yvonne."

"I guess that means her more than us!" muttered Tinker, under his breath.

In the meantime, Rymer had re-entered his car, and was on his way to the Hotel Venetia, where he had made the rendezvous with Hermann Klein in the American bar.

Rymer, for very obvious reasons, had made no mention to Blake of the visit he had received from the ex-convict, nor that Klein was filled with the determination to wreak vengeance on him—Blake—as well as upon John Graves and Mademoiselle Yvonne, for the wrong he believed had been done him in the past.

But even Rymer did not know, when he left Baker Street, that something had happened since he had dropped Klein in Oxford Street which had given an entirely new turn to the plans which had been fermenting in the ex-convict's mind.

He was to learn that when he entered the American bar at the Venetia. As he started to cross the threshold he almost stopped in surprise, for his eyes had already picked out Hermann Klein, now completely rehabilitated, as far as outward appearance went, seated in one corner of the bar talking with another man.

And in that other man Rymer recognised none other than the notorious criminal, George Marsden Plummer.

It was little wonder that Rymer was amazed at the sight of Plummer, for, like most everyone else in touch with events in the underworld of crime, he had heard that, in his last battle with Sexton Blake, Plummer had met his death through the medium of the terrible Death Ray[3] that had come into his possession, and for a fleeting moment it seemed that it must be Plummer's ghost which re-lived in that low club chair in one of the most fashionable hotels in London.

Plummer it undoubtedly was, with certain physical changes, but a Plummer that Sexton Blake, too, would have recognised easily enough. And yet Sexton Blake himself had thought Plummer dead, and must still do so, Rymer was thinking.

It was Sexton Blake and Tinker who had been actually present at what they had believed Plummer's last moments, and it was they who had pronounced the epitaph on the notorious criminal.

Yet there was George Marsden Plummer seated there, alive and apparently in a perfectly normal state of health.

What, could it mean?

Had Herman Klein told him of his intention to wreak vengeance on Mademoiselle Yvonne? Was he seeking Plummer's aid, too?

Possibly Klein had already told this miraculously returned Plummer of his appointment with himself, reflected Rymer. If so, things were going to get a bit mixed.

But, refraining from an attempt to set answers to those questions, Dr. Huxton Rymer moved forward without more than a momentary faltering in his stride, and leisurely crossed the bar to where the couple sat.

---

[3] Plummer's Death Ray (1093) by Nevis Shute.   /drf

WINFIELD GRANGE, the country place which John Graves had bought some two years before, was a good-sized estate in Hampshire, not far over the Surrey border when one passes through Farnham.

The house itself was an old rambling building, part of which dated from Tudor times, and even before Graves took the place over it had been roomy enough. But when, on Sexton Blake's advice, he had kept on the famous training-stables as well—and, indeed, had extended them considerably—he had had a new wing built on to the western side of the house, and now the Grange was one of the real show places in that part.

For the past two Christmas seasons they had gone to Winfield instead of remaining in London, and on this particular occasion Yvonne had planned a larger house-party than usual.

She had not been very enthusiastic when Graves had first proposed au alteration in her scheme to include persons like Huxton Rymer, for there were certain events of the past which had by no means vanished from Yvonne's mind. She could never forget, for instance, that at a time when Rymer had insulted her by trying to force his love on her, he had, in almost the same moment, been intriguing with Prince Wu Ling with the possession of her as the price of the bargain.

When this Christmas proposal had been broached she had wondered if Sexton Blake had forgotten that incident, and had made up her mind that he had.

It was Tinker's enthusiasm more than anything else that won her consent, and once she had given that she spared no pains to see that the list was a well-considered one. She had cancelled a few of the names which she had been considering, and in place of these substituted those put forward by Tinker. It was perhaps on calmer consideration of Yvonne's position in the matter that Sexton Blake had not put forward as large a number as he had at first intended to, and the net result had been that among the number there were only Huxton Rymer and Mary Trent who could be called "doubtful."

From then on Yvonne had appeared far more enthusiastic than any of the others. She left almost at once for the Grange, and organised all the arrangements in her usual efficient way. Graves followed a few days before Christmas, and about the same time certain of Yvonne's own friends also arrived.

The rest of the guests were to turn up on the day before the twenty-fifth. Among these latter were Rymer and Mary Trent, Blake and Tinker. The latter couple had been detained in London until almost the last moment, and it was not until the afternoon that the Grey Panther finally started from Baker Street.

It was in the morning that a startling incident occurred which, had an element of mystery and doubt about it, and which might have had such serious consequences as to throw the party into the gloom of a tragedy. To properly appreciate the occurrence the names of the house-party should be given.

First there were three club friends of Graves', namely, the Messrs. Brownlow, Vickery, and Torrance. Then there was Mrs. Stuyvesant Courtlandt, a very wealthy American woman who had once been a client of Blake's, and owed to him the rescue of one of the most famous collections of jewels owned by any single person. Here was the name on one of the cards which Blake had drawn from the card index, and when it was discovered that she was in London at the time Blake asked that an invitation might be sent to her.

There was a Miss Allenson, a personal friend of Yvonne's, and possessed of considerable means. Next another young woman, a Miss Green, also a friend of Yvonne's, and very poor. She was a protegee of Yvonne's so to speak, and it was invariably Yvonne's care to see that the Christmas season did not find her alone and lonely. Mr. and Mrs. Peter Barnwell, from near Manchester, and formerly known to Yvonne's mother and father in Australia, had come down by car, while others from Blake's list were a Mrs. Travers Orchard and her two pretty daughters.

Then there were as cavaliers for the young women three young men—Captain Brown and Lieutenant Lang from Aldershot, and Mr. Grenside from London. Rymer was to come as Professor Butterfield, and Mary Trent under her own name, but it was to be generally understood that she was Rymer's niece. Then, of course, Blake and Tinker would be there, and finally Yvonne herself and Graves.

Altogether it wasn't a bad sort of list, and in scanning it Yvonne finally concluded that she had arranged it very well. There was the right leavening of young folks, and for the more serious business of bridge or Mah Jong there was plenty of material.

By midday the greater number had arrived, including Rymer and

Mary Trent, but it was just before the latter couple turned up that the incident referred to took place.

After breakfast Graves, accompanied by half a dozen or so of the male guests, went to the stables, a long, rambling pile of buildings about a quarter of a mile from the house. Graves still had a large number of horses in training, in addition to an especially fine collection of hunters, and it was with no little pride that he took his guests over the stables while Henry, his trainer, did the honours of the place of which he had been in command for so many years. (The trainer had been taken over by Graves with the place.)

A number of the guests had chosen to ride, and there were just six in the party that had started out. A good deal of country had been covered in making a tour of Graves' own property, and after that the party cantered along the hard, frozen road into the nearest village, whence it was Graves' intention to return to the Grange stables by a back road.

They kept to this plan, and it was just getting on for midday when the little group of horsemen rode along past the corner by the village inn and turned back towards home.

From there, through one of the paddock gates to the stables, was a matter of a couple of miles or so, and they had covered about half this distance when they rode through the white paddock gate on to Graves' land and entered a small plantation. This wood was made up mostly of pines, which had been planted a good many years ago. They had been put in before the more modern method of wide planting, and as they had matured had thickened considerably.

Now as they passed through the gate Graves had held his horse back until his guests were through. Then he had closed the gate, and on turning his horse found himself twenty or thirty yards behind. He cantered along at a moderate pace in the rear, not troubling particularly to overtake the others.

It was just then, while he was practically alone, that the incident occurred.

Just after entering the plantation the path began to twist, and from time to time Graves lost sight of his companions. He had covered perhaps three hundred yards, and was just mounting a small rise where the growth seemed even thicker than average, when suddenly he felt something rip through the cloth of the cap he was wearing.

Almost at the same instant there came the smothered but

unmistakable sound of a gun of some sort.

Graves had spent too many years in the Australian bush as a young man to be mistaken in that sound. It was a gun. Of that there could be not the slightest doubt, and he was equally certain that a silencer of some sort had been used.

John Graves was an elderly man, but he had by no means grown so stiff in the limb that he could not on occasion muster up some of his old speed of action.

He slipped round the saddle and hung down on the offside of his horse in a way that would have done credit to a professional Rodeo "buster." Then he brought his hand round in a quick slap that lifted his horse ahead on the jump, and in two seconds was round the bend of the path and topping the rise almost on the gallop.

The horse, a high-bred animal who had never experienced such a form of riding, had become nervous at the first strange action, and as its rider still continued to cling to it in the same strange manner it tried desperately to get away.

It might have succeeded in doing so, for Graves was finding the strain of his position almost more than he could continue, but he took the risk after they topped the rise, and just as he regained the saddle found one of the younger men of the party riding back towards him. Graves brought his animal under control, and while the beast was still dancing about saw that the young fellow who had ridden back was Lieutenant Lang, one of the guests who had come over from Aldershot.

"Are you all right, sir?" he asked, reining in beside his host. "I chanced to glance back and saw your horse plunging up the rise. It looked as if you were failing off."

"I'm quite all right," panted Graves. "I wasn't falling off—just doing a bit of trick-riding with this beast—sort of thing I used to do in Australia as a young man. But these English horses don't understand that sort of thing."

The young man looked at him in undisguised admiration.

"My goodness, sir," he said, "I wish you would give me a few tips in that sort of thing! If that is what it was, then you ought to have been in the Rodeo at Wembley. But I really thought your horse was startled, sir, for it seemed to me that I heard the sound of a muffled shot."

The elder man eyed the younger under drawn brows. He had

never met the soldier before, and, to put it truly, had not taken much notice of him up to that moment. But now, as he examined him, he found himself gazing at a clean-cut young man whose steely eyes were full of courage, and who had a shrewd set to his mouth that marked him as a man who could respect a confidence. Graves read him swiftly, and made a resolve just as rapidly. He urged his horse nearer.

"I am going to tell you something, young man," he said, "and I shall ask you to say nothing of what I tell you. You are not mistaken. You did hear a shot. Look here! Do you see the hole in my cap? Well, that was made a few minutes ago by a bullet as I rode behind you up the rise, and it wasn't a bullet of small calibre, either."

"Of course I shall say nothing of this, sir," said the young man, gazing at the hole. "But a bullet of large calibre, sir—I don't understand that. Who could be using a weapon to carry a bullet like that here? There is no game other than birds or rabbits here, and if that bullet was as large as it would seem must have been the case, why—"

"Exactly!" said Graves succinctly. "I do not want the others to know this. I want you to keep guard here for a few moments, and if anyone rides back, say we shall be along shortly. Where I was riding the trees were thick, and I am going to see if I can find the bullet. It is a good chance that it hit one of the trunks there, and I can pretty well get the line in which it came."

Before the other could protest, Graves had turned his horse and was cantering back the way he had come.

It did not seem to occur to him that what had happened once might very well happen again. He was, in any case, a man utterly devoid of fear, despite his sixty-odd years.

He reached the spot where he had been when the bullet nipped through his hat, and there he dismounted. He stood for a few moments getting a line on which way he figured the bullet had come, and then, taking the direction as it had passed through his cap, moved along a few paces until he was close to the trees edging the bridle-path.

A lot of men would have done just the other thing. They would have gone the other direction in search of the source from which the bullet had come. But in doing just what he did John Graves proved himself the experienced bushman who had gone after more than one gang of cattle rustlers and bushrangers in days gone by.

And a few moments later the wisdom of his strategy was proved, for as he moved along, ever so slowly, examining first one pine-trunk and then another, he suddenly halted, and his brows drew down sharply as he saw a chip of white showing against the bark.

He slipped the rein over his arm, and, feeling in his pocket, took out a knife. He opened the blade and prised out the object which had caused the white splinter. It was deeply embedded, but the pine was soft, and he soon had it free. He allowed it to roll into the palm of his hand.

"I wasn't so far wrong at that," he muttered. "A .45 calibre bullet. The probability is that it was fired from a revolver or automatic at very short range. A weapon with a silencer. No one could possibly have any legitimate purpose in this plantation with a weapon of that sort.

"It was an attempt at sheer, cold-blooded murder, and, unless I am very much mistaken, it was meant for me. Well, it missed, and the author has undoubtedly lost no time in getting away."

With that he dropped the bullet in his pocket, and as he remounted he was thinking that, while the young soldier could probably be trusted, there was no object in telling him more than was necessary, and that the subject were best left alone until he could think it over at length in the quietude of his study that night when the others would have gone to bed.

Then, perhaps, he would tell Yvonne— and perhaps he would not.

But, all the same, it was a very disturbing incident, and somehow Graves could not get from his mind the persistent suggestion that it could only be someone well acquainted with the fact that he would be at Winfield who could have made the attempt to assassinate him. He rejoined Lang just then, and evaded any direct answer to the young man's inquiries, merely repeating that he wished him to say nothing about the matter.

They cantered on after the others, and on emerging from the plantation passed through another white gate. Shortly after this the bridle-path crossed the east road that entered the estate from the main London road.

This was the way usually chosen by motorcars coming from Town, and just as his companion crossed it the warning honk of a horn sounded just round a bend on their right. They drew up on the other side of the road and waited to see the vehicle pass.

It came into sight the next moment, and as it swept past something cold seemed to course down the elder man's spine. For at the wheel of the car was Mary Trent, and beside her was Dr. Huxton Rymer.

Graves told himself, as he rode on, that it was, of course, pure coincidence that they should pass just then. But again and again came the niggling thought that if a man had been in the plantation somewhere near the spot where the shot had been fired, he would have had just about time from then to get back to the main road, enter a car, and get as far along the drive to the house as this car was that had just passed them.

And it was the persistency of this thought that made his manner very sombre as he reached the house half an hour later.

Once in the privacy of his own study, John Graves sent a servant with a note to Yvonne, asking her to join him there as soon as she could.

From the branches overhead something hurtled down with terrific force. It struck the top of the wind-shield, and then came full atop of Tinker—a snarling, clawing, biting bundle. (*Chapter 5.*)

YVONNE came within a few minutes, and as soon as she had entered the room Graves motioned for her to close the door.

"Have Rymer and Miss Trent arrived?" he asked.

"Yes, uncle. They got here about twenty minutes ago. Why?"

For answer Graves pulled out the bullet from his pocket and handed it to her.

"Take a look at that," he said. "It is, as you see, a .45 calibre bullet, fired from either a pistol or a rifle—a pistol, I am inclined to think. Now, listen, Yvonne, until I tell you what occurred when I was riding through the lower pine plantation."

Forthwith he began, and related briefly just what had happened, and in what manner he had found the bullet embedded in the trunk of the tree.

"I have said nothing to you," he went on, "but, to tell you the truth, I have not been entirely unexpectant of some attempt being made on my life. Some time ago—two weeks or more, I should think—I received an anonymous letter, threatening both of us. The writer put nothing in the letter by which I could identify him, but it was the sort of document that could only emanate from a mind which was inflamed with some imaginary grievance. I may say, too, that it also contained a threat against Sexton Blake.

"I have said nothing to Blake, for I know that he would ignore it as I have ignored it.

"But this business this morning makes me inclined to connect up the letter with the incident. Of course, I may be entirely wrong, and then there is another thing. I will explain."

Then he told how, just as he and Lieutenant Lang were crossing the bridle-path, the car bearing Rymer and Mary Trent had come along. Yvonne was quick to realise the thought that had come into his mind.

"Of course, it is unthinkable, one would say, that any man could be so treacherous," said her uncle; "but it must be borne in mind, nevertheless, that Huxton Rymer has no cause to love us, and he is a man who can carry an enmity a long time. The point is, just what is the word of such a man worth? Have we been fools to make such a pact with him as we have made to cover the Christmas holidays? Or am I doing him an injustice? Did Rymer write that letter to me before

28

we conceived this Christmas idea?

"I don't want any of the guests to get to know about this, Yvonne. Only Lang heard the sound of the shot, and I have told him just enough to satisfy him. Also, he has pledged his word to keep silent. But I shall not be satisfied until I know whether Huxton Rymer has had a hand in this attempt or not. I wish Sexton Blake were here now. I should like to talk it over with him."

"He will not be here until this evening," said Yvonne thoughtfully. "He telephoned to say that he would be delayed in Town by an urgent matter that had come up, but would get away by this afternoon. All the others are here, and I agree that, for the sake of the girls, this must not leak out.

"But if Huxton Rymer is that sort of a viper, then we must scotch him without delay. I can find out one thing, at any rate, uncle. When everyone is at lunch I can have Alec (Yvonne's chauffeur) go to Rymer's room and go through his luggage to see if he can find a pistol of the calibre which this bullet fits. Alec is, as you know, a past master at that sort of thing, and can soon search everything. Then I will have my maid Anna do the same with Mary Trent's luggage. By the time lunch is over we should know the answer."

"That is a good idea," remarked Graves. "Afterwards we can talk it over again. And in the meantime, don't let this worry you. The spirit of the party must not be spoiled."

And indeed it would have taken a very keen observer to detect the slightest flaw in the gaiety which Graves and Yvonne exhibited before their guests.

The lunch went off without a hitch, and the younger members of the party started off for a long cross-country ramble without the slightest suspicion that anything was troubling their host and hostess. The elder members settled down for an afternoon's bridge (among these being Rymer, Mary Trent having gone with the others for a tramp), and when she had got everyone settled Yvonne made for the study, where Graves was waiting.

"Well?" he asked, as she came in.

Yvonne closed the door and lit a cigarette.

"Alec made a discovery," she said gravely, in a low tone. "In one of Rymer's bags he has found a Service revolver, fully loaded with the exception of one chamber, which, he says, looks as if it had been recently discharged. The odour of burnt powder is still plainly discernible. The calibre is the same as that of the bullet—.45. He found no signs of a silencer, but Anna did find one in Mary Trent's luggage, and it was of the type that would fit a Service weapon such as Alec found.

"Alec had plenty of time at his disposal, and he removed all the loaded cartridges from Rymer's weapon and substituted some from the gun-room, from which he had removed the powder. That is the report, and I confess, uncle, I don't like the look of it. If that shot was fired by Huxton Rymer it is one of the most treacherous acts a man could perform. It also means that the girl is as treacherous as he."

Graves pondered on what Yvonne had told him. Finally he looked up.

"Well," he said judicially, "we can do nothing about it now. The girl is away walking with the others, and Rymer is safe enough at the bridge-table. We shall keep our eyes open and say nothing, and this evening, when Sexton Blake turns up, we will talk it over with him. Now, my dear child, you had better go along to your duties. I shall go into the bridge-room and see that things go along all right there, and, incidentally, I can keep an eye on Rymer.

"That was a good move of Alec's to take the charge from the cartridges in his weapon. All the same, I think I shall take a little life-preserver along with me." With that he opened a drawer of the desk, and, taking out a tiny, flat automatic pistol, slipped it into his hip-pocket.

They left the room together, and while Yvonne went off on her household duties—for the Christmas Eve dinner was to be a big affair— Graves sauntered into the room where bridge was in full swing.

•　　•　　•　　•　　•

It will be recalled that Blake and Tinker had been detained in London longer than they had anticipated. It was getting along in the afternoon before they were ready to get away from Baker Street.

They both sat in the front seat of the Grey Panther, and the tonneau, as well as the luggage rack at the back of the car, contained all the baggage that could be managed. Tinker was at the wheel.

"Let her go, son," said Blake, when he had got a cigar going and had wrapped his fur-lined coat well round him. "See if you can make it to Winfield before dinner. I don't think we need fear any speed hold-ups to-day."

Dinner was the thought in Tinker's mind as he drove along, and it was because his mind was enraptured with that pleasing prospect that he reached the big outer iron gates of Winfield Grange almost before he was aware of it.

In response to the deep siren of the Grey Panther a lodgekeeper appeared and swung open the gates. Then the big car rolled through and took its way along the winding drive towards the house, which was a good quarter of a mile farther on. Like most of the other motor vehicles from town, the Grey Panther took the east road, although Tinker knew that he could have gone by the west road, which branched off just after passing through the main gates.

But the east road was the better, if a little longer, and in a few minutes they were passing the same spot where the bridle-path crossed, and where Graves and Lieutenant Lang had seen Rymer and Mary Trent pass earlier in the day.

It was now past seven o'clock, and Blake was just beginning to congratulate Tinker on the time he had made on the run down when something happened that for the moment threatened to wreck the Grey Panther then and there.

Just what came upon him Tinker did not know then.

He was tooling along at about twenty miles, and looking ahead for the first sight of the lights of the Grange, when, from the branches of one of the trees, on the right of the road something hurtled downwards with terrific force.

It struck the top of the windshield and then came full upon Tinker—a snarling, clawing, biting bundle, with a good sixty pounds' weight or more behind it. In his involuntary attempt to avoid it, Tinker dragged on one side of the driving-wheel, and the Grey Panther shot over the bank and was grinding against the trunks of the trees before the lad, in some sort of sub conscious urge, got it headed back for the road.

In the meantime Blake had lurched up and was already engaged in a hand-to-hand struggle with the thing that had plunged down upon them. As his master dragged the clawing fury away from his face, Tinker managed to bring the swaying car to a standstill, half on the low bank and half on the road.

He was half blinded from the blood that was flowing down into his eyes from the scratches which had been gouged in his forehead, but the strange and sudden attack had put him in a savage rage, and he dived in wildly at the beast, which seemed to have Blake's wrist between its teeth. They had both been at a disadvantage from the weight of their coats, but certainly the thick garments had served to protect them to a considerable extent from the thing's claws and teeth.

As Tinker managed to get his hands about the animal's neck and constrict his fingers, Blake gave a suppressed grunt of pain as the teeth were dragged away from his wrist, tearing at the veins and arteries as they came.

While Tinker ground in his throttling hold, Blake caught up a spanner from the bottom of the car, and as the lad and the beast crashed about, now against the driving-wheel and now against the seat, Blake watched his chance to strike. It came at a moment when Tinker recovered, and by the sheer force of his impetus carried the animal back into the corner of the seat. It fought there like a wild cat, snarling and spitting, while with all its claws it tore and tore again at Tinker's body. It was then that Blake struck.

Once, twice, thrice the heavy spanner descended, and at the third blow the thing collapsed and lay still.

Tinker released his hold, and they both bent down to see what it was that had attacked them.

"A dog-faced ape, as sure as anything!" exclaimed Blake. "Now, what the dickens does this mean? Who on earth in this part of the country can be the owner of such a creature—one of the most savage apes known? Is it possible that it has escaped from some travelling menagerie?"

"I don't know," panted Tinker. "But I'll tell you one thing, guv'nor. That blamed ape was nearly the undoing of us and the Grey Panther. One second more and we would have hit those trees at not less than twenty!"

"I realise that, my lad. How you managed to bring the car back on to the road is a mystery, with that thing clawing at your eyes. It was a devilish attack, and a very strange one. We shall be tough-looking sights to enter Winfield, but that can't be helped. We shall take the body of this beast along and explain things to Mademoiselle Yvonne. But first we had better wipe the blood off each other, or they will get too much of a shock at sight of us. Heave the ape into the back of the car, my lad. I will see if I can find a puddle of water about. But now I remember there is a small stream just a little farther on."

Tinker dumped the dead ape on top of the luggage in the tonneau and climbed out after Blake. He saw Blake in the full glare of the road lamps a few yards ahead, and then, just as he was passing out of the glare, he suddenly paused and he'd up one hand. Tinker drew up also, and then he heard, clear and distinct on the cold night air, the sudden "r-r-r-rat" of a heavily engined motor cycle.

So close did it sound that both knew it could not be very far away. In fact, as they turned and gazed back in the direction of the main road they suddenly saw a light sweep past at high speed. Tinker walked forward until he reached Blake, and then he found something else.

Right across the road, and lying where it would have been seen by Tinker not more than a single second after the attack on him by the ape was a tree, and it didn't need any great amount of deduction to discover that it had been newly felled— felled by sawing through, and not by an axe, in the ordinary way.

Tinker looked at Blake, and Blake looked at Tinker.

"What do you make of this, guv'nor?" whispered the lad at last.

Blake shook his head.

"It is as much a mystery to me as the attack on you—or that motor-cycle which just rushed off down the main road," answered Blake in a low tone. "There is something deeper about all this than at first appeared, my lad. That attack on you—a second more at most and it would have been impossible for you to bring the car back into the road before crashing into this felled tree. If that was pure coincidence, then it is most decidedly a queer one.

"At the rate we were travelling, a crash when you were half-blinded would have been almost certain to prove fatal. That single second is all that lay between us and a very serious accident, or perhaps death. It is entirely due to your quickness of brain and hand that we avoided it.

"But listen, my lad! Doesn't it strike you as odd that we did not hear that motor-cycle until it suddenly roared out quite close to us? If it had been coming along the main road we must have heard it approach, for while we may not have noticed it while we were struggling with the ape, there was a perceptible length of time from when we killed the beast and when we heard the machine.

"It seemed to start at that point, as if someone had had it waiting there and had just mounted it. I confess I am puzzled over this business, Tinker. But we can do nothing now, and, of course, we must say as little as possible about it at the house. It would never do to upset Mademoiselle Yvonne or put her house-party into a panic. We shall get this tree off the road and drive on at once. We shall get hold of Alec at the garage, and then get into the house by a side door. Give me a hand here."

Together they managed to lever the dangerous tree to one side, and then they walked back to the car. They had just climbed in, and Tinker was pressing a tentative toe on the self-starter, when they saw a ghostly figure dash within the outer beam of the headlights. At sight of it they both gave an exclamation, and, despite the wound in his wrist, Blake was out of the car in a clean vault, with Tinker close on his heels. They ran forward towards the figure, and as they drew near Blake cried:

"Yvonne! What is it? What are you doing down this road? Is anything wrong?"

She greeted them laughing, and yet with a strange little catch in her voice.

"I am so glad!" she panted. "I have been so worried about you. I came down to meet you. Why have you stopped? I saw the lights from up the road. Is anything wrong? Why, Tinker—your face is all blood! And you," she cried to Blake— "there is blood on you, too! What has happened?"

BLAKE touched Tinker's hand warningly. Then:

"We had a slight accident, as you see. The car struck the bank, and if it hadn't been for Tinker's quickness we should have had a nasty spill. As it is, we have escaped luckily. There is a little mystery about the accident which I will mention later. But I shall do that at the house. First, however, can you tell me, Yvonne, when this tree was felled?"

For the first time Yvonne noticed the trunk which Blake and Tinker had dragged to the side of the road. She looked at it, a little perplexed frown between her eyes.

"Why, that tree," she said slowly— "I don't know. It was certainly not felled this morning, for I came past this spot during my early ride, and I should have noticed it. No orders have been given for any tree-felling on the estate; and, besides, none of the estate hands are working to-day. But I am sure it has been cut down since this afternoon. I don't understand this. Had it anything to do with your accident?"

"It was full across the road, and we nearly crashed into it," answered Blake.

Yvonne's eyes seemed to grow a deeper violet than usual as she stood in the full glare of the light gazing at Blake. A full minute or more passed before she said:

"I think you are right. We had better talk this over at the house. It is another queer incident in to-day's events. We had better talk everything over with uncle. May I ride back with you?"

"Of course. Will you get in beside Tinker? I shall stand on the running-board. The back of the car is full of luggage."

In this fashion they drove on to the house, and into one of the garages, where the electric light was turned on. As Tinker brought the car to a stop Alec appeared from the shadows outside and saluted the new arrival. Then he moved along until he was close to his mistress, and spoke a few words in her car in a low tone.

Yvonne looked a little startled as she glanced across at Blake, but she said nothing, merely thanking Alec, and telling him to see that the luggage was taken up to the rooms reserved for Blake and Tinker. Then she led the way to a side entrance and up an old, narrow staircase, by which they gained the upper floor.

They followed her along a corridor here until she came to a heavy oaken door at one end which was partially open. Blake knew the Grange well enough to know that this part was one of the oldest, and that the end of the wing terminated in a sort of square tower containing a very comfortable suite of apartments which he and Tinker had occupied on a previous occasion.

"I thought you would like your old rooms," said Yvonne, as she ushered them into the sitting-room, where a cheerful log fire was burning. "Alec will be up with the other men and the luggage in a few minutes. And uncle's man, Peters, will look after you. Ah, here he is now!" Then, to the manservant who entered at that moment: "See after things, Peters. Mr. Blake and Mr. Tinker have had a slight accident. If you will come along presently Anna will give you some dressings and whatever may be needed." Again turning to Blake, she said in a lower tone: "I shall arrange for us to talk things over after dinner." And with that she was gone.

But Blake did not at once go into the bath-room. He motioned for Tinker to do so, and when he guessed Yvonne would have reached another part of the house and had seen Peters depart in search of Anna, he made his way back along the way they had come, and hurried down the narrow staircase to the side door.

He had just got outside when he met Alec coming along with a couple of bags and a bundle of rugs.

"Did you come across something besides the luggage in the back of the car?" asked Blake in a low tone.

"Yes. Mr. Blake. You said nothing about it, so I left it there. What do you wish done with it, sir?"

"Can you manage to bring it up without anyone else seeing it?" asked Blake.

"Yes, sir—of course, sir. I shall slip a rug over it and bring it up next trip."

"What about one of the other men seeing it?"

"I can fix that all right, sir. I can say you have brought it down as part of a Christmas joke, and do not want anything said about it."

"Good! That should serve. I shall get rid of it by to-morrow, but I want it up in my rooms to-night." And with that Blake returned to his apartments.

Blake and Tinker were rather a battered-looking pair at dinner that evening; but Blake had composed a fairly reasonable-sounding tale of their accident, and no one asked any embarrassing questions.

In fact, Blake adroitly kept the subject to Tinker's ability as a driver, and in that way the thing passed off with the usual phrases of sympathy. No particular order had been chosen in the seating of the guests. Yvonne was, of course, at one end, and Graves at the other. On Yvonne's right was old Peter Barwell, and on her left Blake. Graves had Mrs. Stuyvesant Courtlandt on his right, with Mrs. Barwell on his left; and the rest of the order was just as they had gone in, with, of course, Captain Brown, Lieutenant Lang, Grenside, and Tinker well mixed in among the girls.

Graves' friends—Brownlow, Vickery, and Torrance— had also found seats along either side with the partners they had taken in, while Rymer was sandwiched in between Mrs. Travers Orchard—whom he had taken in—and Mary Trent, who had gone in with Captain Brown. Of course, Rymer was known to most of the company as Professor Butterfield, and as both Vickery and Torrance had read some of the erudite articles from his pen, it had not taken long for Rymer to gather some of the glamour of a social lion.

And whatever Graves and Yvonne or Blake and Tinker might be thinking of the pact that had been made, Rymer himself was as urbane and imperturbable as Graves himself. He was geniality personified, and certainly as an asset to the party she had got together Yvonne could not have found one who carried things along better than her old enemy.

For a professor he was a continual surprise, and managed to keep Mrs. Travers Orchard, a somewhat dull and prosaic lady, in a continual twitter.

In fact, everyone at the table seemed in the highest spirits, and as the dinner progressed it seemed certain that Yvonne's efforts were not to be wasted.

The Christmas Eve dinner was, of course, but the prelude, so to speak, of the festivities which she had planned for the morrow, but it was her aim to start the ball rolling that evening and to keep it going throughout the whole of Christmas Day. Her chef d'oeuvre was planned for the following evening, when a party was to come over from a neighbouring country house. It said a lot for the self-control of the girl that, despite the disturbing events of the day, she was as flashingly brilliant as ever—and lovely!

Her dinner frock was some sort of filmy confection which the ordinary male finds it impossible to describe. It was of the material which is known as georgette, and even Tinker would have stamped it "Paris." She wore no jewels except the enormous emerald pendant which Sexton Blake had given her some time before, and the deep lustre of the great stone seemed to sink in like a bottomless pool against the white of her throat. She wore some sort of gold and green band in her hair that matched the green of her frock, and with her well-shaped little head poised on the snowy column round which the great emerald was clasped she looked very wonderful, and very, very desirable.

There were many lovely dresses there that evening, but no great display of jewels. These would be more in evidence on the following night, but as he gazed about him Blake could not help wondering just what Huxton Rymer could be thinking. Then his eyes fell on Mary Trent, and her lips parted against white teeth as she smiled at him.

The last time those two had met had been in very different circumstances, and Mary, at any rate, was capable of seeing the humour of the thing. Blake smiled back, noting as he did so that she looked even more attractive than usual, and decidedly more demure. Then he gave his attention once more to the girl on his right, Miss Green, Yvonne's protegee, and by the time the merry dinner was over had almost forgotten the accident, except for the occasional need of asking Miss Green to assist him at times with his food, for his lacerated wrist was decidedly painful.

After dinner there was dancing and bridge and Mah Jong, and when things were in full swing it wasn't difficult for the four who had arranged the rendezvous to slip away without being noticed.

Yvonne had suggested that they should meet in Graves' study; but just after dinner Blake had a chance to whisper to her that it would be better to meet in his sitting-room, so this was agreed to. Blake had his own reasons for wishing this, but did not say what they were.

He was the first to go up, which was easy enough, as he made a plea that he wished to arrange the bandage on his wrist. Yvonne was the next to follow, and the pair had been talking together in low tones for about five minutes before Tinker slipped in. Then Graves arrived, and as soon as he had entered Tinker closed the door, and all four drew up chairs before the fire.

"We have something to tell you, Mr. Blake," began Yvonne. "It is an incident that occurred to uncle to-day, and it nearly caused his death. I am going to let him do the talking about that. Will you start, uncle?"

Graves' eyes followed the thin spiral of cigar-smoke which was rising from his cigar, then he drawled:

"It was a little startling when it occurred. I will tell you exactly what happened."

Forthwith he began, and related in full detail the incident of the shooting in the pine plantation. Blake and Tinker listened attentively until he came to the point where he and Lang had ridden across the bridlepath just as Rymer and Mary Trent had passed in the car. Then he gave, entirely without prejudice, a repetition of the thoughts that had been working in his mind as he rode on to the stables.

"It is difficult to believe that a man could be so treacherous— even a man of Rymer's type," he said finally. "I am not saying that he had any more to do with that shooting than you or Tinker. I am merely stating the coincidence of his passing, and explaining that it occurred at a moment which would have been just about at the end of a period of time necessary for a man to get through the pine plantation from near where the shooting took place, reach a car on the road, and continue on towards the house, passing that spot as we crossed it on the horses.

"I am not trying to explain anything, but there are three exhibits, so to say. The first is this. It is a threatening letter which I received a little over two weeks ago, and which I put away without giving it any more thought. You will see that it contains a threat against you, as well as against me and Yvonne. Will you read it?"

Blake took the somewhat crumpled piece of paper, and scanned the lines which were "printed" in an obviously disguised hand. It was not a restrained letter in any sense of the word, for the indefinite threats which it made were made to the accompaniment of scurrilous abuse.

"What is the second exhibit?" asked Blake, handing it to Tinker to read.

"The bullet which I dug out of the tree-trunk. Here it is."

Graves handed over the cylinder of lead, which Blake examined, and, after passing this also to Tinker, he found Graves holding out the checked cap which he had been wearing when the shot was fired.

Blake scrutinised the hole which the bullet had made in its passage, and it was plain enough to see just how close Graves had been to death. This, too, he gave to Tinker, and at that point Yvonne took up her part of the tale.

She told how she had sent Alec to go through Rymer's luggage, and how Anna had done the same with Mary Trent's belongings. Blake made no comment until she had finished, and for a few moments after he sat gazing gravely into the fire. Then, without a word, he rose and walked into his bed-room.

He emerged a few moments later, and Yvonne gave a little jump as he dropped on the floor at their feet the dead body of a full-grown male specimen of the savage, dog-faced ape. It was the mysterious bundle which Blake had arranged with the chauffeur to remove from his car. He waited until they had grasped what it really was, then he said quietly:

"Have you any knowledge of anyone in this part of the country who makes it a practice to keep such animals as this as pets? Or might it be possible that there is a travelling menagerie in this part of the country?"

"I don't know of anyone," said Graves.

"Do you, Yvonne?"

Yvonne shook her head.

"I haven't the faintest idea of anyone who keeps apes as pets." she said slowly, "nor do I know of any travelling menagerie in the neighbourhood, although, of course, there may be one. One of the servants might tell us that. Have you looked for any mark of ownership?"

"Yes," answered Blake. "There are no bands about its limbs, and no collar, as you can see. But I will tell you how Tinker and I came to bring such an object into your house."

He reseated himself, and, lighting a fresh cigarette, related just how the savage ape had sprung upon Tinker as they were passing through the plantation. He told of the fight they had had with it before it had been despatched, and for the first time Yvonne and Graves knew how it was they had come by their wounds.

"I was looking for some water to try to make ourselves a little more presentable," he went on, "when, just as I reached a spot a few yards in front of the Grey Panther, I thought I saw something lying across the road. At that same moment I heard the sound of a heavily-engined motor-cycle on the main road at the point which must have been nearest to where I was standing. It went on down the road at a great rate, and I can assure you that neither Tinker nor I had heard it approach.

"I have already considered the possibility that it might have done so while we were battling with the ape, but I shall explain why that does not seem to us to be feasible."

And he did so, using the same words almost which he had used when talking to Tinker.

"We then examined the fallen trunk," he resumed, "and it was easy to see that it had not been felled long. In fact, Mademoiselle Yvonne says that there was no tree lying felled there when she rode past the spot this morning, so that proves that it must have been cut down during the day."

"If it was, then it was done without my authority," put in Graves. "Yvonne has already spoken to me about that. I can assure you that I know of none of my men who would have felled any tree in the plantation, especially on Christmas Eve. I shall, of course, have a look at it in the morning."

"Well, it had been felled by sawing through instead of being chopped down in the ordinary way, and that is a point that might bear investigation. Tinker and I dragged the tree aside, and were just about to resume our way to the house when we saw Yvonne. I did not tell her all then, because I did not wish to upset her or cause any delay to her arrangements here; but after what you have told me about the shooting in the plantation this morning, it seems to me that there is something of a mysterious nature going on about the Grange that must be looked into.

"I know perfectly well that we took a risk when we made that pact with a person like Huxton Rymer. I agree with you that it may have been sheer coincidence that Rymer and Mary Trent passed along the road when they did; but, on the other hand, it is certainly disquieting to learn, from what Yvonne tells us, that there was in Rymer's luggage a weapon of the calibre which this bullet would fit, and that one chamber had been discharged; also, that a silencer to fit that weapon had been found in one of Mary Trent's bags.

"That makes it look—well, rather bad! If Rymer has it in him to be as treacherous as that, then I pledge you my word that this time I shall have not one particle of mercy for him. This whole thing grew out of Tinker's suggestion. People call me a man-hunter—a human bloodhound. They think I would rather see a man behind the bars than save him. They think I would rather punish crime than prevent it. They are wrong—wrong!

"There is a zest in the psychological side of my profession. There is a joy in the little journeys it takes one into the various sciences. There is always the satisfaction of a thing well done. But I have never deliberately hounded a man. I think, in all modesty, I may say that I have given many a man a chance to start anew. And I will confess that, in finally making up my mind to agree to this Christmas pact with Rymer, I was influenced by the spirit of the season. It is a time of forgiveness and peace. If Rymer had it in him to get back to a decent life I was willing to give it to him. But if he has been dog enough to violate this pact in this way, then—"

And Blake gazed grimly into the mounting flames, while Tinker's eyes were shining as he looked at the sombre face of his master; and neither of them saw how wonderfully soft and tender were Yvonne's as she, too, looked at Blake.

"I do not think anyone who knows you can deny the truth of your words," said Yvonne softly. "If a mistake has been made with regard to Huxton Rymer, then it is not your fault. If he can be so treacherous, then he deserves whatever he meets at your hands. I remember—" she went on dreamily, then paused, and her throat crimsoned slowly from where the chain of the pendant encircled it to the tips of her little ears.

Again a brief silence, and it was Graves who broke it.

"There is one thing we have not spoken of yet. It is something Yvonne told me before dinner. It is what Alec reported to you. Yvonne."

Blake glanced up inquiringly.

"What is it?" he asked quickly.

"It is this," she said "After the attack on uncle I determined to keep Huxton Rymer and Mary Trent under observation. When I could not do so myself I had told Alec to do it outside the house and Anna inside. Well, when we drove into the garage after I had met you and Tinker down the road, Alec gave me a report.

"He said that some little time after tea Huxton Rymer had gone off for a walk by himself—that he took a direction towards the pine plantation. Alec followed him, and says that on the other side of the plantation, some two miles from the house, he saw Huxton Rymer meet and converse for some five minutes or more with a man whom he met there. At the end of that time the stranger went in one direction, while Huxton Rymer returned to the house. Who was that stranger? And what had Huxton Rymer to do with him?"

But none of the other three was destined to pass an opinion on that just then, for as Yvonne finished speaking Tinker jumped to his feet, sending his chair to the floor.

The others stared at him, startled. They saw the lad's face working queerly. It was obvious that he was working under some very strong emotion, for his throat was contracted in the actual physical pain of trying to articulate. His eyes were wide and staring, and his gaze was fixed on the window, against which the twigs of a heavy vine could be seen silhouetted.

Blake came to his feet swiftly, and threw an arm about the lad's shoulder.

"What is it, Tinker, lad?" he asked, in concern. "What has upset you? Steady on, now, old fellow!"

Tinker gripped Blake's arm with convulsive fingers. Blake watched him sharply while he tried to master himself, and at last the contraction of the throat muscles passed. He swallowed convulsively; then he burst out, almost shouting:

"At the window, guv'nor—at the window! Plummer's face—and Plummer is dead!"

"What is it, Tinker, lad ?" asked Sexton Blake in concern. "What has upset you ? Steady on, now, old fellow !" Tinker swallowed convulsively and then burst out: "At the window, guv'nor ! At the window——!" (*Chapter 6.*)

"NONSENSE, my lad! At the window? There is nothing at the window, your imagination has been playing you tricks."

"No, sir!" stammered Tinker. "I tell you I saw a face at the window. It was the face of George Marsden Plummer, or—or his g-ghost!"

Blake laughed, and slapped the lad on the back.

"But Plummer is dead, as you know, and as you have said," he urged. "You are thinking of Christmas ghosts, that is all."

But even as he uttered the words Sexton Blake knew that Tinker was too well balanced to get into that extraordinary state over some creepy chimera. And a glance at Yvonne told him that she was far more inclined to give weight to what Tinker said than he.

"Look here," he began, "all this business that has happened to-day, and the talk we have had this evening, is getting on our nerves. Just to reassure you, I shall—"

But what Blake proposed doing was not to be said, for just then there came the confused rush of feet in the corridor outside, and a hurried rapping on the door. Blake swung round, covered the intervening distance in three jumps, and jerked open the door.

Standing there was Alec, the chauffeur, he looked past Blake at his mistress.

"Better come at once, mademoiselle!" he jerked pantingly. "I don't know what has happened, but something has gone wrong downstairs."

And, indeed, as he paused in his speech, the four in Blake's sitting-room could hear the distant sounds of screams— the high-pitched screams of women in terror. Yvonne caught Blake's arm, and even the nonchalant Graves came to his feet.

"This business is getting a bit complicated!" said Yvonne calmly. "What is the best thing to do?"

Blake needed nothing now to urge him into action, he was still in ignorance as to what it was Tinker had really seen at the window, but there was no denying the urgency of those screams that reached them from the drawing-rooms beneath. It was up to him to take command, and he knew it. Something told him in that moment that he was facing one of the most serious crises of his whole career. Uppermost in his mind was the thought that Huxton Rymer had dealt them treachery, and he never wanted anything in his life more than he wanted just then to kill Rymer for this thing that he was doing to them.

"It's outside as well as inside!" he rapped. "Can't tell yet just what is afoot. Weapons—we must have plenty. Get together what men we can depend on. You, Graves—can you count on some?"

"Yes. Lang and Brown, at any rate. Vickery, too old—no use. Torrance for another, and Grenside, I think. Count out Brownlow, but old man Barnwell will fight if he has a gun. Have to get a cordon round the women and stop the panic. What shall I do, exactly?"

"You, Alec!" called Blake to the chauffeur. "Can you get weapons out of the gunroom?"

"Yes, sir—as many as are wanted."

"Good! Then go with your master and get a supply. You, Graves, try to get through to the men you can count on, and for goodness' sake get the women coralled into one room. Alec, as soon as you have been to the gun-room, make for the outside and get together what menservants you can muster. You, Yvonne, go with Graves. Try to get the women under control. I am going outside, and Tinker will come with me. We shall do our work from there, and you can depend that we shall be inside in a short time. And if you see Rymer, Graves, shoot that treacherous dog dead! I have no weapons here. Now go—quickly!"

Alec was already starting, and Graves was close behind him. Yvonne had turned, and had almost reached the door when Sexton Blake turned, and, throwing out his arms, caught her loosely within them.

"Be careful, Yvonne!" he said tensely. "I know it is useless to ask you to stay here, but I shall be anxious about you until I know you are all right. Your greatest danger will be from Mary Trent or others, and we don't know what accomplices may be acting from the outside. That conversation Rymer had at the end of the pine plantation this evening—don't forget that! And now I must go."

His arms tightened till, with a sudden, almost savage gesture, he drew her in to him until her warm breath came up to him in a little choking gasp. She placed her hands against his shoulders, and her wide-open eyes pleaded into his.

"And you," she whispered— "you will be careful, too?"

"Yes. Go, my—my dear Yvonne. We may not pause now."

And yet, despite his words, Sexton Blake still held her close—

tight against his heart, gazing over her shoulder through the open doorway through which she must pass— where? His face came down until it rested against her soft hair; his eyes closed for one brief moment as he inhaled the sweetness of her. Then he drew away. Without a single backward glance he dashed for the door of his bed-room, calling to Tinker as he went.

In his room, Blake tore open a bag and took out a heavy automatic. He looked to see if the clip was in order, and thrust a couple of spares into the side pocket of his dinner-jacket. Then he rushed out again, and saw Tinker just emerging from his room, having been on the same errand. Of Yvonne there was now no sign.

Blake ran to the door and looked along the corridor. He was just in time to see the glorious green blur of Yvonne as she paused at the head of the stairs. He saw her lips move, and he lifted his hand in response. Then she was gone, like a green cloud fading into the black, and Blake turned back into the room. Tinker was already at work on the window, for he had read Blake's intention, and by the time his master was across the room the lad had the sash high.

"Let me go first!" snapped Blake.

Tinker drew back. At the same moment there came the zipp of a bullet past Blake's ear, and a sharp report from the grounds beneath.

Tinker dashed back across the room and slammed his hand down on the electric light switch, plunging the place in darkness and blurring the sharp silhouette Blake's body had made. But Blake was already out on the old vine that grew up the side of the tower, and as Tinker reached the window-sill and thrust out his arm he could feel the vine swaying and quivering as Blake descended.

Another shot—and another—came from below, spattering against the stone. Then as he paused, ready to follow his master, Tinker heard sounds of shouting and shots— it seemed on the same floor as their rooms, he bent out and called down to Blake.

"I believe they are on this floor now, guv'nor. Shall I stay up here and tackle them?"

"No." came Blake's muffled voice. "Stick tight there and be ready to give me a hand. I am coming back."

The vine swayed and quivered more violently than ever as Blake started to climb back again, and a few moments later Tinker caught his hand to help him over the sill. Those below must have expected some such move, for a perfect fusillade of bullets pattered against the stone and through the window. But Blake came over the sill as coolly as he had gone out.

"You are right again, Tinker," he said, as he landed on the floor. "That treacherous devil must have half the loose crooks in London on this raid. It is a wholesale business. Come on!"

He started across the darkened room, but, as he found the door, drew up. Tinker collided with him, and Blake caught him by the arm.

"Listen, my lad," he said hurriedly, "I have an idea of what the strategy may be. That business on the ground floor may be pure bluff. There were no very valuable jewels at the table to-night. If they can be held there in a panic it will give the others a chance to rifle the rooms on this floor. The women will be all right if Yvonne can keep them in one room. Graves and Alec and the others may be able to keep most of the others in hand. But if my idea is correct, the chief actors will get to work on this floor, where the chief booty is. And our work lies here. Follow me. The other wing is our objective. And shoot on sight!"

With that Blake dashed through the open doorway, guided by the light at the other end of the hall. Tinker was close beside him, and together they took the bend by the head of the staircase. As they covered the stretch of another corridor and came into the main part of the building they could more plainly hear the sounds of shooting and screaming on the ground floor.

They rounded the end of this passage and found themselves in the main upper hall, a large, square apartment, with the staircase-well in the centre and the doors of several rooms opening on to it from three sides. At the head of the stairs Blake pulled up and looked down.

In some way the bulbs in the lower lounge hall had become extinguished, but he could see a wide patch of light stretching across the polished parquet, and at the edge of this a twisted figure sprawled. The light, Blake thought, must come from the front room, the door of which he could not see from the head of the stairs.

But he had no time for further conjecture, for at that moment one of the doors on the right was flung open and a man stumbled out. He saw Blake and Tinker in the same instant, and in a flash his gun was up and he was shooting.

Blake and Tinker threw themselves aside, firing in the act.

With a cry the man swung round and went down. But he was not out of business, for, twisting round, he kept on pulling his trigger.

Blake rushed forward just as another door opened and two more bandits appeared. He saw Tinker fling himself past the staircase rail, and saw the pair rush the lad. Then another door was opened, and still two more men came out. And from that moment Blake entirely lost sight of Tinker for a considerable time.

The Eighth Chapter.   Gun-Play.

THE sight of these men bursting from the rooms on the upper floor was all the proof Blake needed that his theory was the correct one.

Back in his own sitting-room the truth had seemed to flash upon him, but here, with the very sight of the bandits in operation, he could get a full grasp of just what was afoot.

It was not particularly new strategy, this that had been employed this evening. It was plain to him that the raid was one of the biggest and best organised of the numerous country house raids which had been attempted for a long time. He could guess now that the number of men employed must be considerable. There was undoubtedly a crowd outside the mansion and two distinct forces at work within— one to keep things in hand on the ground floor, and the other to carry out the actual robbery in the rooms above. So much he saw, and so much he could read.

Who was behind it he could only surmise, and that surmise said—Huxton Rymer.

There was a single shaded light in the upper hall, and the forms of the men who had come out of the rooms were so blurred and indistinct that it was impossible for Blake to see them clearly enough to identify. But so far he had seen none that seemed to correspond to Rymer's big frame. The man who had first appeared had started shooting, proving by this that he knew no others should be on that floor but those who had been told off to carry out the robbery, and that he had orders to shoot on sight anyone else who might show up.

Well, he had done so, and that either Blake's bullet or Tinker's had done its work at last was plain, for after that last spasm of gun-play from the floor the man had rolled over and now lay still.

But the other pair on that side of the hall must also have had the same order? One of them seemed to be encumbered with a sack of some sort, and could not get into action quickly. While he still fumbled for his gun Blake "got" him, and he, too went down.

At the same instant the other man's gun crashed out, and a hot feeling seared across Blake's ribs, just under the left arm, as the bullet touched him. Close work! Another inch would have settled Blake then and there. But he still kept on, and at that the other jerked open a door and rushed back into the room from which he had emerged.

50

But Blake had his shoulder against it before he could close it tight, and with a heave sent it inwards. They crashed together in the semi-darkness within, and as it was too close for gunwork, Blake twisted his weapon and tried to use the heavy butt, he was handicapped by his lacerated left wrist, although he brought it into play despite the pain it gave him.

He was a little puzzled at the lack of energy in the other's resistance after that first rush, and then, without warning, the man slid through his hold and slumped to the floor.

"Got him with my shot, and didn't know it," thought Blake. But he was taking no chances, and although the man lay still, flat on his back, Blake brought down the butt of his automatic hard and certain.

Blake scrambled to his knees, then to his feet.

Now that this first rush was over his thoughts were of Tinker. He backed into the hall and turned warily. There was no sign of the lad, but on the other side of the stair-well balusters lay the body of a man. Blake knew that the lad had been forced to face two, and he was just wondering what could have become of Tinker and his assailant when he heard a terrific commotion on the stairs.

Several figures came up on the rush, and Blake ran forward to head them off. At the same moment he saw Tinker stagger out of one of the opposite rooms. He lurched towards the stair rail and dropped in a heap. Blake changed his course and made round towards the lad, and reached him just as another figure appeared from the same room.

Knowing that it must be this bandit who had apparently "done" for the lad, Blake pulled the trigger of his automatic, but only a "click" sounded. His clip was empty. With a savage snarl he hurled the weapon with all his force full into the face of the man, who was even then taking aim. It caught him clean between the eyes, and he went reeling back into the room again, his pistol exploding harmlessly into the air. By this time the men coming up the stairs had reached the top, and two who seemed to be trying to hold the others at bay were backing round towards where Blake stood. Blake recognised Graves, and then, to his amazement—Huxton Rymer.

Rymer and Graves! What could that mean? How came it that Rymer was fighting side by side with John Graves? He did not pause to solve the riddle then, for the men on the stairs had reached a level where they could shoot, and at the same moment Graves and Rymer drew level with him. Rymer had evidently seen Blake, and was aware that he was now without a gun, for he thrust out a heavy Service pistol.

"Take this. It is fully loaded," he said jerkily.

Blake asked no questions, but grabbed the weapon and ranged himself between the pair. Then he began shooting coolly and carefully, and as first one figure disappeared, and then another, he rapped:

"This is no good. Let's rush them. We can drive them down, and once we get them on the run we have them."

Without waiting to see what the other two would do, he started forward, and from the moment he reached the head of the stairs he seemed to go berserk. He did not even know that Graves and Rymer were close behind him. He hurled himself round the balusters and down the stairs, shooting as he went, and snarling in a fury that drove everything before it.

There were, besides the two men who had been shot down, five more on the stairs; but under Blake's rush they hesitated, and then gave way. By the time Rymer and Graves had rounded the rail they were in full flight, tumbling down the stairs in a wild panic.

Blake kept after them, and as he reached the ground floor caught sight of Alec and a couple of menservants up near the front door, where someone had managed to turn on a light. The fugitives gave pause at the same sight, and swung to the right in the direction of the front room, but they were blocked there by the sudden appearance of Captain Brown and Lieutenant Lang, who came rushing out with levelled shot-guns.

There was another commotion in the direction of the inner hall, and three men came running through from there, headed by one whom Blake suddenly recognised as an American criminal known as Black Gans, one of the worst desperadoes out of Sing Sing.

Black Gans had no intention of surrendering without fighting to the last ditch, he was a gunman by birth and profession, and as he advanced he began shooting as coolly as if the others were so many dummy targets. But Blake had drawn a bean on him, and as Gans shot, Blake's weapon crashed at what seemed the same instant.

For one moment, inexpressibly brief, and yet seemingly an eternity, Black Gans stood just as he had been, his weapon raised and his brain trying to force the message to his finger to pull the trigger again.

The terrible struggle was plainly visible on his swarthy face, and it was still there when he suddenly spun round like a top and crashed to the floor. Blake had got him clean through the heart, and the infinitesimal fraction of a second that he had gained on the drop had placed the bullet there instead of Gans' plunging into his own heart. For Black Gans' boast was that he never missed his man.

As the gunman went down, the desperate spirit seemed to leave those of the bandits who were still in the hall. They were driven back through the inner hall, at the end of which they were taken in the rear by Graves' friends, Brownlow and Torrance. The old Australian squatter, Peter Barnwell, came at them from another side, an enormous six-shooter aimed in a hand as steady as a rock despite his age.

At that they gave in, and, under Blake's direction, no time was lost in disarming and securing them. They were still employed on this work when Yvonne appeared from the direction of the music-room, where she had marshalled the women. After a glance at Blake she hurried back to tell them things were all right.

As for the detective himself, as soon as he saw the work of securing the prisoners well in hand, he turned to go back to the upper floor, where he had last seen Tinker, and as he mounted the stairs a little figure in green came running up behind him. Yvonne just touched his arm, and together they covered the rest of the stairs and hastened round to where Tinker lay. All about them still sprawled the bodies of the bandits who had been shot. Blake urged Yvonne to go down again, but she stubbornly refused. Bending down, she was trying to help Blake lift the lad up, when her arms were pulled gently but firmly aside, and a bulky figure bent over between them.

"This is a job for me!" a voice said roughly. "It may not be as bad as it looks, but if any cutting is necessary I shall do it at once."

And, looking up, they both saw that the person who had intervened was none other than Dr. Huxton Rymer.

Sexton Blake scrambled to his feet. Now that the first rush was over his thoughts were of Tinker. There was no sign of the lad in the hall, but on the floor lay a man. Tinker had had to face two. Where was the other? (*Chapter 8.*)

The Ninth Chapter.   Sexton Blake Asks a Question—and Gets an Answer.

SEXTON BLAKE and Huxton Rymer carried Tinker through to the lad's own bed-room, while Yvonne went back to her women guests.

They made a quick examination of Tinker, and after a complete going-over Rymer came to the conclusion that all that was the matter was a slight concussion due to the shock of a bullet that had furrowed the skull.

He begged Blake to leave him with the lad and to go below, where Graves' old friend, Vickery, was in charge. Vickery, it turned out, had proved to be a retired medical man, who for some strange whim concealed the fact except from his closest friends. Something urged Blake to go, and by the time he reached the ground floor he found some semblance of order being achieved out of the chaos that had reigned.

Graves had already telephoned for the village doctor and constable, and had given the latter sufficient information to send that worthy man into a paroxysm of excitement. He was to get in touch with the superintendent of county police, and also to bring a force of men with him from the village to guard the prisoners.

As it was finally closed, it proved to be one of the biggest hauls of criminals of recent years, with only one or two exceptions. And, although the casualties among the bandits had been terrible, those among the defenders had been comparatively light considering the amount of shooting that had been indulged in.

Sexton Blake was of the private opinion that, if Black Gans had been on duty in the house instead of in the grounds, the result might have been very different, but he kept that to himself.

Nine prisoners in all were taken, while it was figured that six or seven had escaped. There were two bandits killed on the ground floor and four on the upper floor, those four being accounted for by Blake and Tinker. Then, in the terrible struggle he had had in the room on the same floor, Tinker had badly wounded his man before he himself was hit by a glancing bullet. It was the same bandit who had gone down when Blake had hurled his empty weapon into his face. Lastly, there were five bandits severely wounded, while only one of the prisoners was unmarked.

That it was a most carefully organised raid was only too plain. How opportune had been the arrival of Blake and Tinker on the scene was shown when the bags found on the upper floor were opened and the contents examined.

A clean sweep had been made, and, had the thieves got away with their haul, it would have ranked as one of the richest coups known in England. As it was, not a single valuable was lost, and that was enough for Sexton Blake, he made simply a formal statement to the police, as did all the other guests. Nor did Blake mention a single word of what he had suspected of Rymer.

There was a good deal about that phase of it, which he did not understand, and he wanted to get at the bottom of it before committing himself to anything definite. But one thing that did give him a considerable shock was to find that the man he first shot on the upper floor was none other than the ex-convict, Hermann Klein.

He was puzzled over this, and over the fact that of all the bandits he could discover among them not one he could fix on as leader. They were all of the ordinary type which one can scrape together in the underworld for a big job, and were made up or half a dozen nationalities.

Black Gans might have had brains enough to lead the actual raid, but Blake knew perfectly well he had not possessed brains enough to organise it, nor did Klein. Then again would come that thought that Rymer could have organised just such a coup. Had he done so?

Had he betrayed the pact he had made and taken advantage of that to make a clean sweep while a guest in Yvonne's house? And then, when he had seen the tide turning against the bandits, had he in turn double-crossed them, and taken his stand beside the defenders in order to save his own skin?

Rymer was cunning enough to do that, Blake knew. But had he been treacherous enough? *Had he done it?*

That was what Sexton Blake kept asking himself over and over again, and until he knew the answer, he would not be content. And there was just one other thing that still echoed in his mind. That was the cry Tinker had given when he thought he had seen a face at the window of the sitting-room.

"Plummer!" he had cried. And then: "Plummer is dead!"

    .   .   .   .   .

It was nearly the midnight that would usher in Christmas Day before things had regained a normal state—or as nearly approaching that as was possible—at Winfield Grange.

When the police formalities were over, the badly wounded prisoners and the dead were taken off in the cars in which they had arrived for the raid, and which were found —seven of them—in one of the side roads cutting through the pine plantation. Those of the guests who had sustained injuries had been put to bed, and the local village doctor was remaining at the mansion all night.

It was at the very earnest request of the men who had been wounded that the Christmas festivities should go forward, and when the gentler sex had recovered somewhat from the shock of the thing they responded nobly.

Perhaps this was because Mrs. Stuyvesant Courtlandt and Mrs. Peter Barnwell seconded Yvonne's efforts, and by the time they retired to their rooms something like the former atmosphere of the place had been recovered, although each one would have in mind the tragedies which had taken place there that night which was the forerunner of the day which should bring "peace and goodwill" to all men.

Tinker's wound was little more than superficial, and long before midnight he was ensconced in bed as cheerful as ever. And just before the clock struck to herald in the great day an odd little gathering took place in the lad's bed-room.

There was Blake, of course, and Yvonne, her lovely violet eyes shadowy from the stress of what she had been through; then there was Graves and Mary Trent, also looking tired, but with a pathetic little droop to her mouth that made Yvonne suddenly reach out and take her hand. And, finally, there was Huxton Rymer.

It was close on the stroke of the hour when Blake closed the door, and as the silvery chimes of the clock by Tinker's bed tolled out the hour of midnight, all except Tinker rose and stood while the new day which means so much to so many millions of men came into the world. Then Sexton Blake turned to Huxton Rymer, his eyes asking a question.

Rymer looked at Blake; then he glanced at the clock.

"One minute past midnight," he said slowly. "It is Christmas Day. I know what you would ask, Sexton Blake, and I am going to tell you what you want to know —or most of it. And what I speak shall be the truth. Hear me.

"I know what you are thinking—what you are all thinking—except Miss Trent. I don't blame you, but you are wrong. It is not a long tale—let me tell it in my own way. On the very day when I received a telephone message informing me that you wished to see me, Hermann Klein turned up. You all know whom I mean, and you can guess why he came to me. He was down and out as hard as a man can be, but he was filled with one consuming desire—vengeance against you, Sexton Blake, and against John Graves and Mademoiselle Yvonne.

"I listened to his story. I might have helped him in his purpose, or I might not. I honestly can't say now. While he was talking to me the telephone message from you came through. I took Klein to town with me, and on the way I gave him some money—enough to rehabilitate his outward appearance, at least. I dropped him in Oxford Street, making a rendezvous with him in the American bar at the Venetia. Then I drove on to your house in Baker Street.

"You know what took place there. You made what sounded like a fantastic proposal; but it was a sporting offer, and I accepted—on condition that Mary Trent should agree and should also be included in the invitation. On that basis we left it. I said nothing to you of Klein's visit to me or of what he wanted me to do.

"From your house I drove through to the Venetia, and on entering the bar I saw Klein. He was not alone, but in conversation with a man I thought dead, and whom, I have reason to believe, you thought dead as well."

"Plummer!" burst from Tinker's lips.

Rymer nodded, and the lad cried:

"Then it was Plummer's face I saw at the window, guv'nor!"

And both Yvonne and Blake smiled across at him.

Rymer looked a little puzzled at this cross-passage of words, but when Tinker said nothing more he resumed:

"I found Klein in conversation with George Marsden Plummer, and from his attitude I knew that he had told Plummer what he had told me. I joined them, and deliberately, in order to see what effect it would have, revealed what had transpired at my interview with you. Remember, please, that George Marsden Plummer is a friend of mine, and in my dealings with him has always acted on the level, despite the criterion by which you may judge him.

"Well, Plummer was all for taking advantage of the offer you made me in order to arrange a big coup at this house. I would not commit myself until I had seen Mary, and when I talked the matter over with her she would hear nothing of Plummer's plan, although she was all for accepting your offer. As Mary's wishes are more to me than anything else in the world I consented to do as she wished."

Rymer paused there, not looking at Mary Trent. But if ever a woman's soul was in her eyes, Mary Trent's flashed then for the one brief instant that Yvonne saw it. She saw, too, that Mary's eyes were fixed on Rymer in a brooding way that had something of the maternal in it, and a sudden wave of pity and sympathy swept over Yvonne. Sexton Blake glimpsed a little of this, too, but, manlike, he did not grasp its full meaning. The reading of a woman's soul was one thing that was quite beyond Sexton Blake.

"Yes. Mary wanted me to agree to the pact, and I did," went on Rymer. "In the meantime Plummer came down to Abbey Towers in order to lie low, and brought Klein with him. I allowed them to remain, each day they pleaded with me to join in with them, but I would not do so. I'm not trying to pose as a priggish moralist. When this experiment is over we shall— well, we shall see what we shall see. But I had agreed to it, and I meant to stick to it.

"I suspected that Plummer was planning a really big coup, and that Klein was hand in glove with him. That is about all I did know until the night before I came down here. Then they told me the whole truth. I tried to dissuade them, but could not, and, of course, I could not expose them. I talked the thing over with Mary, and she wanted me to oppose it more strongly than I did, but I could not betray an old friend. I could only wait and see what happened.

"Well, we arrived to-day, and this evening I found an opportunity to take a walk and keep a rendezvous with Plummer. He told me then that an attempt had already been made to assassinate John Graves, and asked me if I knew the result. I told him I had seen Graves at lunch, and that he was then in his usual health. He also said that they had scouts out to watch the approach of you, Blake, and Tinker, as you motored down from town, and that they had an unique means of 'getting' you at last.

"I did not ask him what it was. I was, if you understand what I mean, quite neutral over the whole thing. I would not join them, but I would not give them away. I knew when I saw you at dinner, that while their attempt to 'get' you had failed, it had succeeded in marking you.

"Well, there is little more to say. I was looking for the raid all evening, and when it came I definitely made up my mind what I should do. I suppose that was on account of Mary. At any rate, you know that I did make my stand on the side of my host and hostess, but I am sorry for those who met such a tragic fate—and I am glad that Plummer made good his escape. I will not be a hypocrite over the matter. That is all I have to say except that as I have made the pact so shall I stand by it."

As he finished Blake suddenly got to his feet, and, walking across to where Rymer stood, put out his hand.

"I owe you an apology," he said abruptly— "an apology for the treachery I thought of you, and gratitude for what you have done to-night for Tinker."

And as Huxton Rymer took Blake's hand his shoulders straightened. The two men gripped hard, and then, as Yvonne and Graves came forward to do the same, Rymer, for the first time since he had begun to speak, looked full into Mary Trent's eyes. And in that moment he, too, saw the flash of a woman's soul, and he would have been a clod if he had not realised something of the love that was in that soul for him.

And just then, from somewhere in the distance the sound of joyous bells came echoing sweetly across the still, frosty air, ringing out the joyous message of Christmas.

THE END.
[23100 WORDS]

With **Xmas Greetings** to all U.J. readers, old and new, and sincere wishes for your good fortune in our several competitions.

The Editor

61

The MYSTERY of the MARSHES

A brilliant new Serial of Gun-running Adventure on the
Essex coast, by - - - - - - - H. W. TWYMAN.

The Mystery of the Marshes

A brilliant new Serial of Gun-running Adventure on the Essex
coast, by H. W. Twyman.

The First Chapters in Brief.

BOB CASTLE and his cousin, JIM POLDEN, are two young
smacksmen engaged in the work of oyster fishery, and living in the
village of Merwell, on Mersea Island.

They decide to try to bring to justice a gang of men, headed by an
unknown foreigner, who are smuggling arms to Germany or Russia,
and who have already captured Jim, whom they suspected of spying
on them.

Jim has been rescued by his cousin, however, and by a ruse the
gun-runners have been made to believe that they are dead.

On their return to Merwell Jim goes to Colchester to keep out of
the way of the innkeeper, who is in the plot. During a conversation
with his uncle (Jim's father) Bob learns that gun-running is suspected
by the Coastguard Service, and reveals what he knows.

The talk is overheard by a youth named Adam Sperrit, a
notoriously crafty fellow, who has been listening outside Bob's
cottage. When he goes Bob sets out after him, intent on finding out
what he has heard.

He leaves his uncle, whom these events have made comically
mysterious, at the gate of the cottage, promising to keep "his weather
eye lifting."

(Now read on.)

"WHAT'S come over the old boy all of a sudden?" the youngster asked himself, as his uncle gazed after him from the gate. "Acting just like a stage villain! However, this affair'll give him something to think about, that's dead sure. Brighten up his existence no end. Coastguards along this river don't get so much excitement that it gives 'em 'that sinking feeling'!"

Ten minutes of walking brought him to the village, where he looked in at the oilshop-garage for a sight of the heir to the business. But young Adam was obviously not on the premises. Without waiting to question his father, who was serving a small girl with some treacle, he passed along the High Street in the expectation of meeting him before long.

What he intended to say when he did meet him he had not yet troubled to think. Young Sperrit was a very doubtful proposition, and would have to be handled warily. He might purr like a cat, or scratch like one.

Bob was walking steadily along the main street of the place, with an eye lifting towards the cottage doors to catch sight of his quarry if he should be delivering orders, and conning over in his mind how he had best tackle his bit of cross-examination, when he found himself approaching the village green and the Ketch Inn which stood opposite.

As he looked up at the building, with its cheerful, green-painted windows and its swinging sign, he saw the person of whom he was in search.

From out of the passageway at the side of the inn Adam Sperrit emerged suddenly, facing in his direction. There was a triumphant look on his face—a look as of a praiseworthy deed accomplished—until he in turn caught sight of Bob. Then that expression vanished, so unexpected was the encounter, and momentary dismay took its place.

He had come from the inn, the watcher realised; from the very alley-way where Bob himself had gone the evening before in search of his missing cousin, and where he had found that mysterious men had been drinking in the shuttered lift! Amery Gurr, the landlord, must have known of those men. What business had this scared-looking young eavesdropper just had with Amery Gurr?

Bob Castle strode towards him. The other stopped in his tracks, gulping down his surprised panic and assuming a counterfeit grin.

"Here, Sperrit," said the young smacksman, "I want a word with you!"

"I'm busy, but you're welcome," replied the other, smiling but uncomfortable.

"I won't keep you all day!" retorted Bob. "I don't want to delay you getting back to the 'garridge.'"

"What is it, then?" demanded Sperrit. His face was gradually recovering its wonted assurance as he conquered his surprise.

"What were you doing at the Ketch?" snapped Bob.

"What's that to you? What d'ye think I was a-doin'—robbing the till?"

Bob ignored the latter sarcasm, and continued:

"Tell me now, and quick! What were you doing in there? Did you go to see Amery Gurr?"

"For sure."

"Ah! And what—"

"Deliverin' orders, if it's got anything to do with you, which it hasn't! Taking him some candles he'd ordered. What about it?"

Bob Castle paused and stared the shifty-eyed Sperrit searchingly, wondering how he could get around his plausibility. Something seemed to tell him that there was more in this visit than candles.

Just then he became aware of a cycle-bell, furiously jangled, immediately behind him. He turned quickly, and was just in time to jump sideways as a boy on a bicycle came hurtling towards him, and, with both brakes jammed on hard, came to a sudden and spectacular standstill on the spot where he had been standing. It was young George Marney, the boy-of-all-work from the Merwell Post Office.

"What's the hurry?" exclaimed Bob, as the youngster swung himself nimbly off the bike. "Isn't the road wide enough for you?" He was rather nettled at this rude interruption of his interview.

"Not goin' any farther!" replied the lad. "Telegram for ye. Caught sight of ye as ye passed the post-office, so I didn't waste time goin' up the road to your cottage."

As he spoke he produced a specimen of the familiar, brownish-coloured envelope that denotes a telegram, and handed it over. Merwell had a telegraph-office, but it did not boast overmuch traffic, especially on behalf of local smacksmen such as Bob Castle.

"You've got to go to Colchester," the boy volunteered with a grin, as Bob tore open the envelope and began reading the message inside.

"Oh, you've been reading it, have you?" queried Bob.

"Saw it come through," explained the other laconically. "Any reply?"

Bob nodded his head negatively, and the messenger mounted his machine with a flourish and pedalled away as if he were engaged in a sprinting race. Young George Marney was one of the few live wires of the placid village, and habitually did everything at the double. Thus early in life he affected the urgency of the man of affairs, and nurtured secret ambitions of becoming a merchant prince and coming back one of these times to astonish the natives.

Bob Castle frowned in annoyance as he read the telegram. It was from his cousin, Jim Polden, in Colchester, and he realised that, in such a small and gossipy place as Merwell, it was going to be no easy matter to keep his existence a secret. Luckily Jim himself had realised this, too, and had refrained from signing the wire. It simply read:

"Meet me town-hall four o'clock."

The "office of origin" was stated plainly enough as Colchester, and Bob knew without the help of a signature that the sender was his cousin.

He thrust the slip of paper and its envelope in his pocket and turned to confront Sperrit again. But that slippery youth had already taken his chance and vanished—probably back into the Ketch, where Bob did not care to follow him. He could be attended to later, the young smacksman reflected, as he eyed the front of the inn frowningly.

Meantime, he had better be getting off to Colchester for this appointment with Jim. There was none too much time, and it must have been something of importance to have induced his cousin to telegraph.

He made his way along the High Street till he came to the church, from outside which an occasional bus makes the journey inland to the market town. He was unfortunate in that the next would not be departing for another fifteen minutes, so he filled in the time by walking along to one of the village shops and buying a packet of cigarettes and a London newspaper.

With these he returned to the bus and mounted to the top, where he proceeded to light up and read till the bus should start.

Almost the first news item that caught his eye was the following:

"MYSTERY MOTOR-CAR. ABANDONED ARMS ON ROAD-SIDE.

"Late last night a motorist, driving a private car along the main London-Chelmsford road just north of Brentwood, almost collided with a stationary van, the front wheels of which overhung a ditch by the roadside.

"Suspecting an accident, he examined the vehicle, and found it to be apparently abandoned. The van was loaded with stout wooden cases, and there were several spots of blood near the driver's seat, which may have resulted from an injury caused when the car left the road.

"The Essex Police were notified, but no trace of the owner or driver of the car has yet been found, nor have any witnesses come forward who saw the accident. An examination of the load showed that the cases, which were unmarked, contained machine-guns, rifles, and ammunition.

"It has been found that these cases are not the usual ones provided by the makers of the firearms, who cannot account for this consignment being repacked, or suggest any likely destination.

"The number-plates of the van had been removed prior to its discovery, as had also the police licence card. The Essex Police are anxious to trace the owner of the car, and also any witnesses who may have seen the accident or noticed the driver passing through Brentwood or London.

"In view of the present case of alleged gun-running with which the London police and Custom House authorities are engaged, it is believed that this abandoned van may furnish an important clue."

Bob Castle read steadily through the paragraph, and then let the paper fall to his knees and stared steadily ahead in tense abstraction.

Gun-running!

Once again the word had cropped up. There must be something at the bottom of these suspicions. There must be! Whatever lurking doubts he may have had about his cousin's suspicions of the crew of the mysterious Vandervelde, the overlooked Lewis gun bolt which Jim had picked up in her cabin could be capable of no other explanation now, far-fetched as it had seemed.

Then, too, there was the matter of which his uncle had told him— the equally mysterious lorries that made their nocturnal way to the lonely Thancastor Chapel, overlooking the even more lonely mudflats of the Blackwater River.

This abandoned van found full of machine-guns on the main Colchester road—may it not have had some connection with the mystery? It was probably what it seemed—an accident and consequent disablement, and a hasty retreat of the occupants before they were discovered.

Then there was the mention of a case of gun-running in London itself. This was the first he had heard of it, for he was by no means a regular reader of the metropolitan dailies, and the word gun-running had held no particular significance for him until the previous evening—a short twenty hours ago. Bob realised dully that it seemed a much longer time ago than that so much had happened in the interval. And with the reflection came the realisation that he was tired. He had been up all night, and worked up into a tensity of excitement most of the time, too.

His head gave a jerk as the bus suddenly started, setting out on its eight mile journey. Soon he would be in Colchester; a little more than an hour, and he would know why it was that Jim wanted to see him so urgently.

A Decision —and a Disaster!

THE hands of the clock in the tower of the town-hall were pointing to the quarter after four when Bob climbed down from the bus-top, scanning the pavement below for a sight of his cousin.

There were several passers-by moving past the spot, but it was plain to see that his cousin was not among them. Bob walked across the stretch of intervening roadway and along to the portico fronting the muncipal building, but Jim was certainly not there, for he glanced into every nook in which he might have been standing.

"I'm a quarter of an hour late!" he muttered. "Not my fault, of course, that the bus was so slow. But perhaps he's given me up already. Got impatient or something. Or perhaps he might have been seen by somebody from Merwell, and got out of the way."

Whatever the reason, Bob decided he would wait there at the rendezvous till his cousin turned up. At any rate, he would give him a clear hour, and then seek him out at the Harveys' house, at which he knew he was staying. It would be injudicious to go there before that, he surmised, or his cousin would have asked him to call there direct.

It was well that Bob Castle decided on a policy of patience, for he stood or sauntered about the precincts of the town-hall for a full hour, and ten minutes in addition, before Jim Polden kept his appointment.

He sidled up in a secretive way that was very foreign to his usual bluff manner, coming upon Bob from behind.

"Sorry, old chap!" he said, with a glance in each direction. "Couldn't get here before. There's been a fellow hanging around. Come on! This way!"

Without further explanation he gripped Bob's sleeve and gave it a tug intimating that he was to follow him. He dived abruptly into a narrow side street on which the town-hall abuts, turning, and beckoning with head in a way that Bob found both curious and unmistakable.

"This is getting like a regular moving-picture drama!" thought the young smacksman, as he grinned to himself. "First Old John, with his stage-villain antics, and now Jim's got 'em!"

He caught up with his cousin when they were well out of sight from the main street they had left, and demanded to know what was "up."

"Sorry I kept you waiting so long," apologised Jim again. "It would have been too risky for me to venture out sooner."

"Risky?"

"Yes. There was a man hanging about outside the house where I'm staying. He was on a job of shadowing— shadowing me. But he wasn't exactly a Sexton Blake at the game, and it was quite plain what he was doing. All the same, I couldn't risk showing myself, or coming openly to the town-hall, because the house is in a quiet street, and he would have been sure to have spotted me. It wasn't till I waited an hour that I found out I could get over the back garden wall and into another street."

"But what's all this business of shadowing and such like?" demanded Bob. "How do you know he's after you? Who is he? I reckon this gun-running business has gone to your head, and you're imagining things."

"No such luck!" retorted Jim, as he led the way along the street at a brisk pace. "Anyway, what do you make of this?—A car drove up while the man was waiting, watching the Harveys' place from the opposite corner, and it stopped for somebody inside to speak to him."

"Did you recognise the car" asked Bob.

"No; but it was a Ford, with the hood up."

"How about the driver? Did you see him"

"I tried to, and I think—only think, mind you—that it was young Sperrit."

"Sperrit! Are you sure?"

"No; I said I wasn't. I was watching from behind a thick curtain. Anyway, it looked like him, and his father certainly has a couple of old Fords in his garage. What he could have been doing there, though, beats me. Perhaps it was somebody else, after all."

"Most likely it was him," put in Bob gloomily.

"What makes you think that?"

"I'll tell you later. Let's come somewhere where we can talk. And, oh, by the way, why did you want me to meet you?"

Jim glanced ahead and astern (as he would have expressed it), and then, when he saw they were in no danger from eavesdroppers, he produced something from on inner pocket, folded it, and held it before his cousin, with a finger pointing.

It was a newspaper, and it was folded at a paragraph headed: "Mystery Motor-Car."

"Oh, that!" said Bob, with a note of disappointment in his voice. "I've seen it."

"Have you? It doesn't matter, anyway," replied Jim Polden. "In any case, this affair makes a difference to our plans, so far as I can see. Don't you see, this thing is altogether bigger than we thought. There are no two ways about it—we'll have to tell the police what happened last night. It's only right that you should have a say in it, though! and, besides, there's a lot to talk over."

"Let's go to the castle grounds, then," suggested Bob. "We can be quiet there."

Jim agreed with a nod, and they turned off in the direction of the famous old castle, whose enormous, time-defying walls date back to the time of the Roman invader and the later Norman, and which are situated in a pleasant park.

There, in the peace and quietude of the gathering dusk, the two young smacksmen talked together of the many things to which Jim's startling adventure of the previous evening had given rise, the only sign of their presence as the dusk merged into night being the low tones of their voices and the dim shape of their figures on the bench on which they sat.

It was now obvious to them both that the situation had changed— or, rather, that they had known only of that part of it which concerned themselves. They had neither of them been aware that there was a London end to this gun-running business, for their work together during the past few days had been too strenuous to allow them to assimilate all the contents of the papers, and if there had been any report about this affair they had missed it.

Now, however, Jim Polden had had time to make inquiries of the people with whom he had been staying in the town, and also to read various week-old papers that had been lying about. And in the meantime they had both read the latest item of news concerning the abandoned lorry.

"There's no doubt about it now, Bob," said Polden. "What we know is only a part of the whole thing, and the London police probably know a good deal more about it than we do."

"But they don't know the part that we know," rejoined Bob.

"Maybe not; but seeing they already know something, it's up to us to tell them."

His cousin nodded his agreement, and for a time the two puffed at their cigarettes in silence. It was not till the low rumble of their talk resumed again that a lurking, vague shadow, among the hardly less deep shadows of a jutting buttress a few yards from the bench on which they sat, began to move, any slight noise it may have made being covered by the sound of the conversation. It sidled cautiously along in the gloom under the old wall, and presently was lost to view—had anybody been aware of it—round an angle of the building.

A few minutes passed, during which the two cousins on the bench, unconscious of any listener, talked on. Then the crunch of their feet on the gravel announced that they had risen, and were moving towards the gateway that gave access to the street.

"That's that, then!" Bob Castle was saying. "We'll go straight to the police-station, and tell 'em all we know."

"Reckon they know it already, maybe." put in Jim.

"Maybe they do, and maybe they don't. Won't do any harm, anyway. It's got wonderful dark while we've been in here talking," he added inconsequently, as they emerged into Museum Street.

His cousin nodded absently. It was a decisive step they had determined upon.

They had judged it best, in view of the official knowledge of what was going on, to abandon any intention of tackling the gun-runners single-handed. They realised that, although their knowledge of local conditions, and the Blackwater estuary in particular, would be of value to them, the knowledge of what was happening there would also be of value to the police. It would mean, too, that Jim could come out of hiding and show himself in Merwell. Even if the crew of the Vandervelde had the hardihood to return there and attempt to molest him, there was the comforting thought that the police would not be far behind.

They had gone a matter of five minutes' walking, when Bob suddenly hesitated in his stride, pulled up, and went back a pace or two. He stopped, and leaned forward slightly, peering at something white on the wall of a dilapidated shed. Jim turned and retraced his steps, too, wondering what it was that had attracted his cousin's attention.

It was a small poster, or, rather, a handbill. The top line, printed in heavy black lettering, read:

"£50 REWARD."

Underneath was a fairly large halftone reproduction of a photograph of some sort, and beneath that again some lines of small type.

"What's this?" muttered Bob. "Fifty pounds reward!"

"Looks like a police notice," suggested Jim, bending forward.

"So it is! Here, hold on a minute!"

There was the rattle of a matchbox as Bob dived his hand in his pocket, and a moment afterwards a glare as he struck a light.

"Why." exclaimed Jim excitedly, "it's —it's the man I saw aboard the Vandervelde—the boss of the gang! He went aboard from the Ketch Inn! It's the same chap—the very same! Just a mo'! Let's read what it says. 'Whereas'—keep the light steady— 'Whereas, on the fifteenth instant, Julius Griff, at the Bow Street Police Court, in the County of—'"

He stopped. The match had gone out, burned down to Bob's fingers. Jim turned impatiently to watch him strike another. There was a sudden soft scurry of footfalls on the pavement near by which neither of them paid any particular attention to in the absorption of the moment.

Then, without the slightest warning, Jim staggered one way and Bob another. Their knees collapsed under them, and they reeled and slumped to the ground, the concussion of the double fall quite audible in the stillness of the street.

Two men immediately seized them, one grasping Bob by the shoulder, and the other his cousin. An elongated, indistinct shape dangled from the right hand of either—a shape that a better light would have revealed as a sandbag, with a looped thong slipped over the wrist.

They wasted no time on conversation. The street, though now deserted, might at any moment produce a witness to their deed. Luckily for their purpose, it was not a main street. Directly the eyes that had watched the lads' every step from the castle grounds had seen them turn into this short cut, the opportunity had arisen.

Without a moment's delay first one and then the other backed down a little alleyway between the end wall of the shed and the wall of an adjacent garden, dragging his burden with him. The heels of the unconscious comrades scraped limply and waveringly over the stones as their bodies were drawn backwards, and then rustled through the coarse growth of damp weeds and grass that flourished in the alleyway.

The walls were no more than two feet apart, and it was quite dark in here. The two assailants, indeed, could neither of them see the other.

"All right?" whispered the last to enter, in a husky growl.

"Ay!" came the reply from the man who was further up the alley.

"Tap 'm on the bean if they get frisky," recommended the husky one. "You know what to do. Wait 'ere! We'll soon 'ave 'm outa this!"

There was the rustling of his feet among the luxuriant weeds, and he became visible to his partner in the alley as a silhouette peeping round the edge of the wall up and down the street. Presumably the coast was clear, for he stepped out into the open and vanished silently to the left.

The man on guard bent down and gingerly ran his fingers over the face and head of the one he had accounted for; it happened to be Jim. The face was cold, and now that the attacker's eyes had become used to the darkness, could be seen as a dim white patch against the ground. It was white enough, in all reality. He was quite insensible, for the deadly sandbag had done its work effectively; but he was not dead, as the man was relieved to find when he groped his way to the youth's chest, and felt the slow beat of his heart.

He grunted his satisfaction at work well done, and crawled along to the second victim. Bob, too, was in much the same state as his cousin.

Rising cautiously to his feet, the man detached the loop of the sandbag from his wrist, and slipped the weapon in his trousers-pocket, and then crept nearer the opening into the street, where he leaned nonchalantly against the wall and waited. There, save for the movements necessary to slip a piece of chewing tobacco in his mouth, he remained motionless, until he heard the distant sound of a motor-car, when he became alert.

He refrained from exposing himself, however, until he knew by the sound of wheels grating against the kerb near by that it was the car he expected. As the vehicle came to a stop opposite the alley, there was the sound of someone descending from it, and next moment his husky-voiced accomplice slipped into the opening in front of him.

"Where are ya, Shorty?" he whispered. "Ah, right away! This one first. The street's clear, but if anyone shows up the lad's going to blow the hooter. Got 'is shoulders? Right! Lift! Mind you don't drop 'is cap, or anything!"

"Ay, ay!" came the response, and the pair shuffled towards the street and across the pavement. The springs of the car gave a sudden creak as the burden was half pushed, half hoisted into it.

The driver, who seemed in the darkness to be but a youth, and slightly built—did not look round at them, but kept his eyes darting up and down the length of the street.

"All clear!" was all he said.

Thereupon the process was repeated, and once more the leader and the man whose sole vocabulary seemed to consist of "Ay, ay!" emerged from the dark alley with a sagging burden.

The unconscious Jim was stowed partly alongside and partly atop of his equally helpless cousin. One of their assailants got in the front seat alongside the driver, and his taciturn friend climbed in at the back, covering his knees, and incidentally the two youths, with a brown Army blanket.

There was a whirring of gears, and the car started forward.

And had anybody been there to notice, it might have been observed that it was a Ford car, rather battered, and with the hood up.

(Whither bound now? What is in store for the two chums—or the gun-runners? Next week's instalment will tell. Don't let things slide—order now!)

Choose books as Christmas presents for yourself and your pals this year. There is nothing else which gives so much entertainment at so low a cost.

There arc two splendid books now on sale at all newsagents and booksellers which will interest for months to come. Their titles are the "HOLIDAY ANNUAL" and the "CHAMPION ANNUAL." You will want to read the stories in them, not once, but many times over.

The "HOLIDAY ANNUAL" is packed with amusing and thrilling stories of the adventures of a group of well-known schoolboy characters— Harry Wharton, Tom Merry, Jimmy Silver, Billy Bunter, etc., from the schools of Greyfriars, Rookwood, and St. Jim's. Besides the stories, which are well illustrated, there are many articles dealing with hobbies and games.

The "CHAMPION ANNUAL" is a big budget of adventure yarns. In every line there is a thrill. In this breathlessly exciting book you will follow intrepid heroes as they work against overwhelming odds in all corners of the world.

Remember the names of these topping books — the "HOLIDAY ANNUAL" and the "CHAMPION ANNUAL," price 6/- net each.

An Account of the Sensational **PADDINGTON GREEN MYSTERY.**

An Account of the Sensational PADDINGTON GREEN MYSTERY.

The Paddington Green murder of 1836 was a remarkable affair in many ways, not the least being that it anticipated in almost all its details the equally notorious crime of Patrick Mahon over eighty years later. Its horror was magnified by the fact that it occurred at the season of peace and goodwill.

REMARKABLE was the Christmas of the year 1836 in the North of London. For many years it remained a memorable one in the minds of that generation, to be involuntarily recalled, with a shudder, each recurring Christmastide. It was marked out from all others not only because of the cold weather and the heavy fall of snow which marked its arrival, but for the ghastly and cold-blooded crime which was committed on the eve of that Christmas Day.

Exactly where the murder was carried out, and by whom, was not discovered for some time afterwards; even the crime itself was not brought to light until a day or so after it had taken place.

It was on December 27th that a snow-shoveller, pursuing his task of clearing away the snow from the buildings in Edgware Road, discovered a large sack by the roadside. It was filled with something, and its neck was tied tightly with rope. The snow-sweeper, after making a few guesses at the contents of the sack, endeavoured to lift the curious bundle, which he found was extremely heavy, passing his hands over the bulky form of the contents as he did so.

To his horror, he found that the sack contained a human body! There was no mistaking the form and the lines. It was undoubtedly the body of a grown-up person.

Murder!

The horrified thought, coming as it did at the Christmas season, appeared even more gruesome.

The police were soon notified, and the sack with its mysterious contents was carried away to be examined. In it was found the body of a woman. The head and legs were missing, and the arms were tied together with twine.

An old towel, marked with the initials "J. C. B.," and a child's blue frock were wrapped round the body. The frock had been patched with a piece of nankeen, a material much used for children's clothes at that time. There was also a quantity of wood shavings, clotted with blood, in the sack, and a length of cloth, which was afterwards found to be part of a carpenter's apron.

Here were several clues upon which the police could work in their efforts to find the perpetrator of this ghastly crime, but their first task must be to identify the body.

After an exhaustive examination the police doctor gave it as his opinion that the body was that of a woman between thirty and forty years of age, about five feet six inches in height, and of fair complexion.

Hers had been no lingering death, he suggested, but one that had overtaken her suddenly, as intimated by the absence of blood from the vessels in the body. It was hazarded that death had been caused through a blow on the head or through the throat being cut.

The dismemberment of the head and legs had been done in a very amateurish way—certainly not by a skilled surgeon.

That was all that could be ascertained until the missing portions of the body were found, and the police set themselves assiduously to this task.

It was by no means an easy one. The whole of Edgware Road and the Paddington neighbourhood were combed for a clue, but not another vestige was discovered there. Nor was there any help forthcoming from the avalanche of reports of missing women received by the police. One after another these reports were investigated, but the decapitated body was not identified by any of the relatives of missing persons.

Some time elapsed in these fruitless investigations, and the case looked as if it would have to be added to that long list of "Unsolved Mysteries," when an explanation was suggested.

Explanation and Sensation!

Could the affair have been a joke? someone asked. Had the body been dismembered by a young medical student, perhaps, and left in the road for a joke —a grim joke certainly? Or had some midnight grave robber performed the deed?

The former idea was scouted, but in lieu of any better clue, the suggestion of the grave-robber might be worth following up. Accordingly, the police made inquiries from churchyard and graveyard authorities in the neighbourhood as to whether any opening or rifling of graves had taken place.

But this led nowhere, and investigations along that line were soon dropped in the light of a new sensation that occurred in the middle of January, 1837.

A woman's head was discovered in the Regent's Canal. The finder was a bargeman. and in working his craft through a lock in the Stepney part of the canal had hooked up this gruesome article with his barge-pole.

It was found by the police doctors to belong to the unidentified body, and a search for the missing legs was now begun.

The discovery of the head in the canal had inclined the police to the belief that the crime had been committed by a bargeman, and it was to the canal that they now directed their search. More than a mile of the bed of the waterway in the Milo End district was dragged without any result.

It was then suggested that the murder might have taken place at Paddington, where the body was found, and that the head was taken on a barge down the canal and dropped at Stepney. Accordingly the northern end of the canal was subjected to dragging operations— equally without results.

The Sack Clue.

The body was still unidentified. The head was very disfigured, and the features had become almost unrecognisable through the long immersion in water; and although the murder had caused a great sensation in London, the identity of the murdered woman remained a mystery.

Had it not been for the timely discovery of the missing limbs and the assistance of a man named Gay, it would probably have been a mystery to this day.

It is a far cry from Edgware Road to Coldharbour Lane, Brixton, but a field in the latter neighbourhood was the scene of the next sensational find. Tied up in a sack in the same way as the body had been, a pair of human legs was discovered by a labourer.

The bundle had evidently been lying in the grass for some weeks, and upon examination the limbs were found to correspond exactly to the missing portions of the mysterious body.

A further search in the sack revealed some shavings similar to those which accompanied the body. This positively linked up the discovery of the Brixton sack with that found at Paddington, and there remained no doubt in the minds of the police that a callous murder had been committed, and that the murderer had used this method of scattering the evidence of his crime.

But they were still confronted with the task of identifying the body and tracing the murderer.

A further clue, furnished by some letters which were printed on the sack found at Brixton, was followed up. This led the police to a brewer who lived at Camberwell. He recognised the sack as being one that he bought some years before, together with a number of others. More than this he could not say. Every sack of that batch had left his possession in one way or another, but when and to whom each one went it was impossible to discover.

Three months had now gone by since the finding of the dead body, and as every avenue had been explored, and every clue followed till it petered out, there seemed to be nothing more the police could do.

Public interest in the affair had waned through lack of material to keep it alive, and newer mysteries had already ousted the Christmas murder from the front page of the Press, when a sensational development occurred.

The woman's body was identified.

One Half Solved

This was about the end of March. Among the reports which were still straggling in from persons who were seeking news of missing wives, mothers, sisters, etc., was one from a Mr. Gay, of Goodge Street.

Like all the other suggestions, this one was thoroughly investigated, but unlike those that had gone before, this one led straight to the murdered woman, and was at last the means of solving the Christmas murder mystery.

It was two days after Christmas that a snow-shoveller discovered a large sack in the snow by the roadside.

The man Gay informed the police that he had a sister named Hannah Brown, who had been living at Union Street, near the Middlesex Hospital. For some three months now he had heard nothing of her, and upon inquiring at her lodgings had discovered that she had not been there since the previous Christmas Eve.

On that day Hannah had left her rooms in the company of a man named Greenacre. He was reputed to be her fiance, and the unfortunate woman had confided that she was soon to be married to him.

Since that Christmas Eve all trace of her had been lost, and although Gay confined that he and his sister had not been on very friendly terms, he felt constrained to do all that could be done to solve the mystery of her disappearance.

The police, with their side of the mystery still on their hands, took up the inquiry immediately. Mr. Gay was conducted, as so many others before him had been, to the place where the body could be seen. After the first shock was over he had no hesitation in identifying it as that of his unfortunate sister.

One half of the mystery was now solved, and with the name of the man with whom the victim was last seen in their possession, the police had hopes of soon being able to lay their hands on the murderer.

Unpopular!

That marvellous system of police organisation was set in motion, and it was not long before Greenacre was found, living in a little street in Lambeth. With him were a woman and their child, a girl of about five years of age.

At first the man indignantly denied all knowledge of the murder; but after a search of his residence had been made, bringing to light a child's frock patched with the identical material as the patch on the frock found in the sack, he was arrested.

The woman, Sarah Gale, was also arrested as an accomplice, and the pair were taken to Paddington Green Police Station.

There were no Black Marias in those days. The usual method of conveyance in such cases was by hackney cab, and in one of these more or less open vehicles the two prisoners were driven to their destination.

Police-officers accompanied them, and somehow the connection between the brutal Christmas murder and these two in the cab must have been discovered or guessed at by the public, for a howling mob followed the procession.

Shouts and booings were directed at the prisoners, and some even attempted to pull them out of the cab. The presence of the two limbs of the law acted as a sufficient restraint, however, or it may have gone hard with the suspected pair.

Arrived at last at the comparative quiet of the prison cell, Greenacre—a good-looking, intelligent man of about fifty years old proceeded to concoct a "statement" that would clear him of the terrible charge against him.

He and Hannah Brown were lovers, he wrote in this confession, and were intending to be married on the Christmas Day of 1836. On the eve of the wedding he had called for her at her lodgings, and together they had travelled to his house at Camberwell.

It was discovered later that Sarah Gale had at this time been living at that address, but she was away from the house on the Christmas Eve.

Patrick Mahon's Prototype.

Arrived at his home, so the statement continued, he and Hannah Brown had sat down to have some supper, and had talked about money affairs. Hannah had said that she was possessed of some few hundred pounds, and on this evening her intended husband had pressed her to tell him where the money was, and when she could get hold of it.

The woman was drunk, he continued, and laughed hilariously when he persisted in his questions about the money, confessing at last that she had been lying to him, and that in reality she was quite penniless.

This so enraged the prisoner, on his own confession, that he gave Hannah Brown a push by way of protest at her deceit. To his consternation, he saw her fall off her chair, striking her head against a log of wood that was lying on the floor.

He went to her assistance, but found that she was already dead.

The thought of the construction that would be put upon this unpremeditated action so terrified Greenacre, according to his statement, that he took immediate steps to cover up the deed. Dismembering the body, so as to make the disposal of it less difficult, he had deposited the portions in the various places from where they had since been removed by the police.

That was the story offered by the Christmas murderer—a story which, it will be realised, is similar in many details to that to be put forward by Patrick Mahon, the Eastbourne murderer, some eighty-eight years later.

Evidently Greenacre was dubious of its deceiving anybody, for a few days later he was found hanging by the neck in his cell, and was only cut down just in time to save his worthless life.

Four months after this, in July, 1837, Greenacre and the woman Gale were brought to trial at the Old Bailey, charged jointly with the wilful murder of Hannah Brown. The man had all along stoutly denied that Sarah Gale had any hand in the affair, or had even known of Hannah Brown's visit to the Camberwell house, but various pieces of evidence went to disprove this statement.

The trial was one of the most spectacular and thrilling which had ever taken place at the Old Bailey. Public interest had been roused to an enormous degree by the utrocious crime, and vast crowds clamoured at the doors for admission long after the building was filled to overflowing.

There were no free seats in the public gallery in those days. Seats were usually charged for, like the seats in a theatre gallery, at the rate of a shilling each.

At the trial of Greenacre, however, the price was raised from one shilling to ten-and-sixpence. But even at that price every seat could have been sold several times over. The excitement was so intense that crowds of fashionably dressed and influential people thronged the doors, endeavouring to get a glimpse into the court.

A howling mob followed the prisoners . . . Some even attempted to pull them out of the cab.

Disproof

When the two prisoners were brought into the dock a strange contrast was to be seen. Greenacre, calm and self-possessed, took up his position and quietly surveyed the crowd gathered to witness his trial for life.

He had none of the appearance of a guilty murderer, and throughout the whole trial his audacity and nerve upheld him. He had evidently dressed with as much care as if he were attending a Court function. The fancy waistcoat and blue coat gave him a fashionable appearance, which was well carried off by the smart black stock he wore. Here again the resemblance to Patrick Mahon's case will be immediately noted, for the recent Eastbourne murderer "got himself up" in much the same way, even going to the extent of tinting his face with some artificial sun-tan mixture to make him more attractive.

The woman, on the other hand, was drooping, dejected, and visibly trembling from the moment she entered the dock. Not once during the proceedings did she voluntarily raise her eyes to cast a look at the people thronging the well of the court.

There was a hush as the judge and jury took their places. Greenacre's statement was read, and the prosecution proceeded with their part in the trial.

There were many flaws in the prisoner's "confession," counsel pointed out. For instance, expert medical evidence had proved three things which were quite contrary to the statements made by Greenacre.

Firstly, that there had been no trace of alcohol in the woman's stomach; secondly, that her throat had been cut before death; and thirdly, that she had been dealt a severe blow on the front of the head, and not on the back.

This disproved three of the prisoner's sworn statements.

Additional evidence had also been gained in the meantime, to the effect that the sack found at Paddington had been stolen about a week before Christmas by Greenacre from the man who owned it, a cabinet maker named Ward.

Here again the case foreshadowed that of Patrick Mahon. In his trial also it was proved that, as the means of disposing of the body had been obtained some days before the death of the victim, the murder was premeditated.

Nemesis.

Greenacre's statement that Sarah Gale knew nothing of the crime was again subjected to argument. Prisoner was living in the same house as Gale at the time of the murder. It appeared hardly feasible that he could have manufactured a sufficient excuse for getting her out of the house while he lured the other woman there, robbed her— as he had obviously intended to do—murdered her, and had disposed of the body.

There was also a suspicious circumstance in the fact that Sarah Gale was wearing jewellery and clothing belonging to the dead woman; and, what was even more conclusive, she had been identified by a pawnbroker as the woman who had accompanied Greenacre when he had pledged a travelling-bag belonging to Hannah Brown.

When the counsel for the prosecution sat down, and the defending counsel rose to make his speech, there was not much doubt in the minds of the twelve good men and true as to what their verdict would have to be, and the exhortations of the defence did not do much to shake that decision.

It was urged by defending counsel that Greenacre should be found guilty of manslaughter only. There could have been no murder, as there was no motive for murder, pointed out the attorney. Prisoner was very fond of Brown, and had, in fact, arranged for the banns to be called so that they could be married on Christmas Day.

Taking all this into account, persisted the counsel, it was quite probable that prisoner's statement about the accidental fall was the truth.

That was all. It was a lame defence; but after all, there was not much to be said in favour of so callous a creature who could lure a woman to his house and murder her in cold blood on Christinas Eve.

In view of the doctors' evidence, the jury found Greenacre guilty of murder, and the perpetrator of the brutal crime was sentenced to death, Sarah Gale being transported for life.

Christmas Crackers.
A Present From the Cells.

SANTA CLAUS stockings, or Christmas presents of any sort, are not very plentiful in prison.

The warder in Los Angeles County Gaol was surprised, therefore, when he found himself the recipient of a bulging stocking last Christmas.

He was more surprised still when he untied the fastenings and examined its contents. There were no toys or sweets; no whistles, or Jack-in-the-boxes; not even the usual orange. All he found was a collection of small saws—some with handles, and some without.

But, coming as it did from some of the prisoners in his charge, this gift spoke volumes. Pinned to the stocking was a note, which read: "As a true observance of the proper Christmas spirit, we herewith present our compliments because of the kindness that has been shown to us in the past.—*THE MEN IN TANK NO. 9.*"

One of the donors had been chosen as spokesman for the party, and when presenting this strange gift to the warder he explained the reason for it.

The little party in No. 9, he said, had decided to make their getaway from the prison. They had obtained the files secretly, and had succeeded in sawing away parts of the iron bars from their cells. The preparations were almost concluded, in fact, when Christmas intervened.

The spirit of goodwill, usually associated with this season, together with the reluctance to play such a dirty trick on the warder who had been so considerate to them, had caused them one and all to change their minds.

Hence the gift, which, though the most unexpected, was probably the most treasured of any the prison official had received—and the strangest.

Christmas Camouflage.

It was Christinas night, and a children's party was in full swing.

Squeals of mock terror and shrill screams of laughter, mingled with the deeper tones of merriment from the adults, caused a din that could be heard for some distance.

The scene was in the Clerkenwell neighbourhood, and the fun and excitement were taking place in a large building which had been converted into model dwellings.

Out on to the landing ran the children, and up and down the stairs, dancing with glee, tearing off one another's paper masks and hats, and altogether having an hilarious time.

On the lowest floor of the building lived an elderly man, alone, and while the unsuspecting children were frolicking above, the man was being murderously attacked down below. The happy laughter of the children was so loud and prolonged that when at last the man's feeble cries were heard it was too late to capture his assailants.

It appeared that while the basement dweller was sitting alone in his room, enjoying a quiet Christmas, he heard someone trying to open his window. He thought it was some of the children intent on playing some prank, and called to them to go away.

The man's disturbers were not children, however, but three men, who very soon found a way into the house and down into the basement, where dwelt the solitary man. They broke open the door of his rooms and attacked the occupant.

The victim of these Christmas intruders shouted for help, but the cries were drowned by the revelry and shouting above.

At last some neighbours who had heard the cries and had thought they emanated from the children, decided to go and investigate.

They found the man unconscious upon the floor, badly wounded on the face and head, and hastily summoned an ambulance and had him removed to hospital.

The Story of London's Police

A series of five absorbing articles telling of the birth and development of the world's finest police force, from the time of the old Watchmen to the present-day Policeman.

Part Three.—The Coming of the "Bobbies."

The Story of London's Police

A series of five absorbing articles telling of the birth and development of the world's finest police force, from the time of the old Watchmen to the present-day Policeman.

Part Three.—The Coming of the "Bobbies."

SOME sort of measure of peace and order was maintained in the City of London, as we have seen in the two previous articles in this series, by various bodies of so-called police, long before the outskirts of the City of London, or of the towns of the provinces came to be effectively patrolled.

From time to time Acts of Parliament were passed for the improvement and regulating of the City police forces. And the citizens of the City thought they had achieved a mighty thing when, in 1737, they brought pressure to bear on their Members of Parliament and got for themselves an enlarged and improved force of— 68 men!

It was not long, naturally, before that force was found to be entirely inadequate. How could 68 men, aided by a few "old Charlies," maintain law and order over the one square mile of the congested City of London?

Eventually it was remodelled, the Lord Mayor and aldermen taking the job in hand, and so improving the skeleton force that by the year 1838 the numbers had mounted to 501.

It was that police force, organised and maintained by the City of London, that Sir Robert Peel took for his model when he established the Metropolitan Police Force. That body was intended to preserve law and order in that part of London outside the City area. The amazing part of it all is the astounding opposition which was levelled at him from practically all parties.

Sir Robert Peel, founder, in 1829, of the Metropolitan Police.
[Illustrations from prints in the Mischgitz Collection.]

Members of Parliament howled him down when he rose to speak on this topic in the House. They took their cue from their constituents, who were practically unanimous in declaring that this new move on the part of the Home Secretary, Sir Robert Peel, was the thin end of the wedge of Prussianism.

A drilled and organised body of fit and able men, such as Peel's force of police would be, was something entirely new for the citizens of London to contemplate. The men could be used to oppress them. At any time this threatening force might be let loose to ride roughshod over London. Such was the trend of public thought when Sir Robert introduced his Act for improving the police.

However, the Act was jostled through Parliament and became law. And so there appeared on the scene the "Peelers," otherwise "Bobbies," both nicknames bearing on the surname of the man responsible for their assembly.

To say that they created a sensation when first they trod the beat is to put it very mildly. In the first place, their costume was scarcely dignified. The most conspicuous feature of a "Peeler's" make-up was a tall, stove-pipe hat. A policeman in a topper!

It was ever so shiny, too, and very black, in contrast to the blue of the tight, brass-buttoned uniform, with its stiff stock pressing hard up to the chin. Which gave rise to the mocking cry of rude little boys and loafing hobble-de-hoys when they saw a Peeler or Bobby in the distance:

"I spy blue, I spy black—

"I spy the man in the shiny hat!"

The new police were recruited from the ranks of the several distinct bodies then playing at safeguarding the London streets. The rival local police authorities, with one exception, came into line with Peel's force, the Bow Street Patrols and others being absorbed at once into the Metropolitan Police.

But the City Police stood out. It was Peel's great wish to incorporate that body with his young Metropolitan Force, but the City would have none of it. They desired nothing so much as to be left alone as a distinct organisation. And they had their way.

Against any consolidation of the two forces—the City Police and the newly formed Metropolitan Police—the Corporation of the City of London advanced four chief reasons, the most powerful one being to the effect that the City so differed in its locality and the nature of its property from other parts of the Metropolis as to require a separate and differently regulated police force for its protection.

A Bill was passed, in 1839, authorising the City to continue to regulate its own force, which it still does to-day, the City Police Committee seeing that various Acts concerning their police are put into execution, though disciplinary matters are under the control of the Commissioner, who in turn is directly answerable to the Home Office.

Under his command there are now approximately one assistant commissioner, three superintendents, six chief inspectors, twenty-five inspectors, seventeen sub-inspectors, 103 sergeants, and over 1,000 constables, excluding nineteen constables on private service duty.

The upkeep of the City Police now costs over £435,000 a year. The area patrolled by them is, roughly, 675 acres in startling contrast to the beat of the Metropolitan Police. This extends over a district comprising well over 447,000 acres, with a population exceeding five millions.

It reaches from Cheshunt in the north to Chipstead in the south, and from Chadwell Heath in the east, to Staines in the west. The Metropolitan Police district contains the whole of the county of Middlesex, and the parishes in the counties of Surrey, Hertford, Essex, and Kent of which any part is within twelve miles of Charing Cross, and those also of which any part is not more than fifteen miles in a straight line from Charing Cross, except, of course, the City of London.

The force is also employed in his Majesty's dockyards and

military stations far beyond the Metropolitan Police district.

The Metropolitan Police, whose head office is at Scotland Yard, costs close on £7,000,000 a year, and the world agrees it is worth every ha'penny spent upon it. It justly shares with the City Police the encomium passed on the latter body by Lord Mayor Phillips, who declared it to be "the most civil and the best civil force in the world."

But all this did not come about with smoothness. Sir Robert Peel had a gigantic task before him in forming the working skeleton, as it were, of the Metropolitan Force. He could not get the City Police to act as its backbone, though the new body absorbed the Thames Police.

Weeding out the Force.

The best he could do in the circumstances was to weed out the least useful members of the ancient forces he was endeavouring to mould into one properly-organised body, and to build up on the remainder. As it happened, the remainder was not much good, either.

Wholesale dismissals occurred from the new force during the first year of its existence, either on account of arrant dishonesty or physical incapacity. The total number of throw-outs during the first twelve months was three thousand.

A typical Peeler, forerunner of the London policeman, in his work-a-day dress.

The old Charlies, parish beadles, and all the other varied servants of the law before Peel's advent on the scene with his scheme, had their own peculiar ideas of honesty. The same rotten principles were carried into the new force.

Urchins in the streets, anxious for a catchword to hurl at the Peelers, seized with delight on the opportunity given them when one of the new force was run in by a fellow Peeler for stealing a goose from a poulterers shop whilst on duty.

For months after every Peeler was greeted from afar with gleeful shouts of:

"Bobby, Bobby, let me loose;
You're the man that stole the goose!"

There was little enough inducement for the right type of man to join the force. The pay was a miserable nineteen shillings a week. The real matter for wonder is not that acts of dishonesty occurred, but that they should have occurred as seldom as they did when once Sir Robert's scheme got into smooth working order.

Up to the time of the foundation of the Metropolitan Police, the local forces of law and order were generally so little trusted that business men sometimes paid private forces of their own to guard their property and interests.

A classic example of that sort of thing is, of course, the eighteenth century incident of the Tyburn hangman. He was not a policeman, but was no less intimately connected with the law. They arrested him whilst he was carting a condemned man to Tyburn Tree. And a bit later they hanged him on his own gallows.

As recently as 1914 there was a serious case of wholesale thefts on the part of a number of the police at a certain seaside resort. But those lapses are so extremely rare nowadays that when they do occur they impress themselves vividly on the minds of those who read about them—more vividly, maybe, than the accounts of the decoration of police-constables for conspicuous gallantry.

The discipline maintained is of the highest possible standard. It has kept pace with the gradual evolution in dress, so that the "bobby" of the present is as superior in every way—intellectually, physically, and morally—to the old "Peelers" as it is possible to conceive.

Then again, compare the mounted police of 1924 with the ancient Bow Street Horse Patrol! The old patrol was but a handful of indifferently disciplined and trained men mounted on old cavalry horses. Now the London police numbers, roughly, three hundred mounted constables in its ranks.

That is a development fit to rank by the side of the Police Electric Motor Ambulance System. Inaugurated by the City Corporation in 1907, with one motor-ambulance, stationed at St. Bartholomew's Hospital, the system has rapidly developed until now there is a regular fleet of police ambulances stationed in readiness to rush to the scene of any street accident.

And, of course, every constable is taught First Aid, as they are schooled in many other matters pertaining to their manly calling.

The most recent development concerns the formation of a small force of women police. So far as London is concerned, their job is more on the lines of rescue and child-welfare work than anything. There are twenty-four attached to the Metropolitan Police, but, so far, there is none working with the police of the City.

All told, the number of women "bobbies" in England and Wales is 110, but only about one-third of them are empowered to arrest anyone.

A London policewoman—a recent and very successful innovation in the war against crime. [Photo: Topical]

The Metropolitan Policewomen are attached to various divisions, and are not, as they were at first, controlled from the "Yard," though one of the two police-women inspectors is attached now to the Criminal Investigation Department of Scotland Yard.

The job presents so many attractions that there is at present a long waiting-list of applicants eager to become women "bobbies." Which state of affairs is strikingly different from the prevailing rate of recruit merit for men police.

Though, when we come to look into the figures, we find that it is not that there is a dearth of willing recruit to the Police Force, but that the physical standard of more than ninety per cent of would-be policemen is too low to allow of them being admitted to the ranks.

It is interesting to compare the rates of pay and conditions of service in the London police. To take the newest branch first. The pay of a woman constable begins at £3 per week, rising by two-shilling increases each year to £4.

A woman sergeant gets £4 10s. to commence with, rising to £5 per week, with uniform and boots provided. The women police do not live in barracks, but are "billeted" at home. They get one day's leave in seven, with ten days off by way of an annual holiday.

The pay of the Metropolitan policeman ranges from £182 a year, the wage of an ordinary constable, up to £1,000 a year for a chief constable. Sergeants get from £260 up to £320; inspectors, from £326 to £553; and superintendents from £550 to £775.

Those sums can be supplemented by the smart officer—not in the fashion followed by the pre Peeler police, but by honest work within the Force. Outside the Force, officers are strictly forbidden to engage in any work "other than employment sanctioned as Police Duties by the Home Secretary."

Extra money comes a smart man's way through special employment at Headquarters, as a short-hand writer or storekeeper. And then there is an additional detective allowance to be earned, ranging from an extra five shillings a week for constables to fifteen shillings a week for superintendents.

Naturally, this magnificent and wonderfully efficient police service—whose birth we owe chiefly to Sir John Fielding, that famous old blind Bow Street magistrate, and Sir Robert Peel, its actual founder—costs the City and the Metropolitan area a very large sum annually.

This is raised by a rate of about one shilling and a penny levied on every pound of rental. In this way the various districts pay for the police according to their means, the wealthiest paying most. A vastly different state of affairs, this, from the days when odd men were privately employed to guard the goods of the wealthy, and the poor were practically left to look after their own goods and chattels!

The upkeep of the Metropolitan Police is assisted considerably by the hire of policemen by ordinary individuals and Government departments. Last year the police earned in this way the respectable sum of £681,000, paid mainly by the Houses of Parliament, the Royal Navy, and the British Museum.

Then there are various licences which help to swell the police coffers, and last year nearly £70,000 went into the police bank by way of fines inflicted on "visitors" to the various police-courts in the metropolis.

As the Force has grown, so have the duties increased in volume and complexity. The old "Peeler" had a sinecure compared with the job of the present day "bobby." Not only has he to be an encyclopedia of general knowledge, which he is expected to dispense at a moment's notice to whoever demands information in the streets, but he is also expected to have at his finger-tips, as it were, the contents of the Police Book.

Between the covers of that thick book are listed all the duties that fall to the lot of the policeman, with rules of conduct for his guidance. Unquestioning obedience to superior officer; ranks in importance only to the command contained in the words, "Whatever duty you may be called on to perform, keep a curb on your temper."

In those two tenets lies the secret of the tremendous success of the London police. A man who can obey an order without hesitating an instant to inquire why or how is the fittest to command himself and win the respect of others. In that latter respect, the constable finds his greatest help in his difficult job.

For even the lowest of East End hooligan has a sneaking respect for the stalwart officer who runs him in. And in a difficult situation, the one who does not lose his temper stands a ninety per cent chance of coming out top-dog, whether it be in a "rough house" or in the diplomatic handling of a hostile crowd.

The use of handcuffs is discouraged by the police authorities, and it says volumes for the capability of our London "bobbies" that the sight of a handcuffed man is one of the rarest; few people have ever seen handcuffs in use.

Muscle and brawn help there, as they help in a thousand other eventualities But the exercise of "brawn" is hedged in and limited by official rules.

If it were not so, the narrow boundary between persuasion and Prussianism would be in peril of being broken down; and then would arise the very condition which the enemies of the "New Police" legislation of Sir Robert Peel professed to stand in dread of.

The constables that supplanted the "old Charlies" would have been appalled had they been faced with one-fiftieth of the duties of the "bobby" of to-day.

Roughly, these can be summed up under such heads as the maintenance of order among traffic and pedestrians, the suppression of begging, the prevention or prompt removal of nuisances and obstructions, the rendering of First Aid to the ill or injured in the streets, the enforcement of by-laws relating to the public health, the prevention of juvenile smoking, and, to round off this very condensed list, the apprehension of wandering lunatics.

After twenty-five years of endeavouring to do all those things and countless other thankless tasks, the constable retires on a well-earned pension.

If he happens to be incapacitated from further police service by reason of injuries received in the execution of his duty, the State either awards him the usual pension or, if he has served less than fifteen years, a gratuity.

Pensions are also awarded to the widows and children of constables who are killed "in harness." Fortunately, these fatalities are few. The training of police recruits is directed vigorously to the dodging of an early demise.

A motor police ambulance, one of a swift fleet maintained by the City Police.
[Photo: Topical.

In the King's Name!

It may be news to some that refusal to aid a policeman when called upon is punishable by imprisonment and fine. The official "book of words" says the constable in need of such assistance shall call on anyone in this wise:

"In the King's name. I call upon you to assist me, a police officer, in the execution of my duty, to convey this person to the police-station."

That appeal, though, is as scarce on the London streets as the handcuff episodes previously alluded to. The police-whistle is perhaps heard more often, but even here the pride of the ordinary self-reliant constable, grappling with big odds, prevents him resorting to this shrill summons for assistance. In many cases, when the whistle is blown, it is by some courageous passer-by; even women have been known to rush into a melee, grab the battling constable's whistle, and blow until reinforcements arrive on the scene.

Another dissimilarity in the terms and conditions of service as enjoyed by the "Peeler" of the past and the "bobby" of to-day in the prospects of promotion to really well-paid posts. The old "Peeler" had nothing but a life of hard knocks to look forward to if he was without powerful friends who could bring influence to bear in the right quarters. The policeman of the present has the "Yard" to aspire to.

If every soldier carries a field-marshal's baton in his knapsack, so every constable has his chance of being picked out for promotion to the ranks of the detective force. How the ambitious and successful "bobby" joins up with Scotland Yard will be related next week.

Bow Street Police Court, once the headquarters of the Bow Street
Runners and the old Patrol—forerunners, respectively, of Scotland
Yard and the Mounted Police. [Photo: Topical.

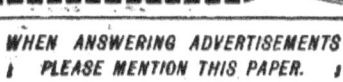
97

£10 a week for LIFE, or— £4,000 "Cash Down"!

SECOND PRIZE £300 FAR & NEAR £200 THIRD PRIZE

A SPECIAL NEWSAGENT'S PRIZE of £50 to the newsagent who supplies the FIRST PRIZEWINNER with his copies.

PUZZLES AND FULL PARTICULARS OPPOSITE

Complete List of Names for reference throughout this Great Contest. Every name denoted by "Far and Near" pictures is in this list, somewhere.

CUT OUT THE LIST AND KEEP IT.

Acre, Acton, Aden, Adrianople, Avadir, Aisne, Alabama, Alaska, Albany, Albemarle, Albert, Alderney, Aldershot, Alexandria, Algiers, Alhambra, Alliance, Alps, Alva, Amazon, Amber, Amiens, Amritsar, Amsterdam, Ancre, Anglesey, Angora, Antrim, Antwerp, Appledore, Aragon, Ararat, Arc, Arcadia, Archangel, Argentine, Arizona, Armentieres, Arras, Arrowhead, Artillery, Arundel, Ascot, Astrakan, Athens, Atholl, Atlantic City, Auburn, Auckland, Aurora, Austin Friars, Axminster, Ayr, Azores, Babylon, Badminton, Bagdad, Bagshot, Bakewell, Balaklava, Balmoral, Baltic, Baltimore, Banbury, Bannockburn, Bantry, Bapaume, Barcelona, Barham, Barnet, Barnsley, Barth, Battersea, Battle, Bay City, Beachport, Beaver, Belfort, Belgrade, Belmont, Belvedere, Benares, Bengal, Bentworth, Berber,

Bergen, Bergland, Berlin, Berkeley, Bermudas, Berne, Bethune, Bidwell, Biggleswade, Bigtimber, Billingsgate, Birchtown, Birdhill, Birnam, Biscay, Bisley, Blackfriars, Blackpool, Blanes, Blenheim, Bloomsbury, Blue Nile, Bluff, Boatman, Bohemia, Boom, Bordeaux, Borneo, Boston, Bosworth, Botany Bay, Braemar, Bray, Brass, Bremen, Brigg, Bright, Brightlingsea, Brightview, Brindisi, Brisbane, Brittany, Broadway, Broken Hill, Brooklyn, Brussels, Bucharest, Buffalo, Bullecourt, Burghead, Burgundy, Bushire, Bushmills, Buxton, Cadiz, Cairo, Calais, Calcutta, Caldwell, Calgary, California, Callao, Cambrai, Cambridge, Camden, Campbell, Campbellton, Camperdown, Cannes, Canterbury, Canton, Canvey, Cape Town, Cardinal, Cardwell, Cargo, Carleton, Carlsbad, Carolina, Carthage, Cashmere, Cawnpore, Cayenne, Ceylon,

Champagne, Chanak, Charing Cross, Charly, Charm, Charter, Charterhouse, Chatsworth, Cheapside, Cheddar, Chelsea, Chicago, Chiltern, China, Chipping, Chislehurst, Chorley, Cintra, Circle, Clacton, Clashmore, Clearville, Clerkenwell, Cleveland, Clones, Cloudy Mount, Clovelly, Clydebank, Coleman, Colenso, Cologne, Colombo, Colorado, Columbia, Coney, Congo, Copenhagen, Corfu, Corinth, Cork, Corral, Corsica, Corunna, Cossack, Cotehill, Cottesmore, Cowes, Cressy, Crete, Crimea, Crewe, Crowes, Croydon, Cuba, Culloden, Cyprus, Damascus, Danube, Dardanelles, Dartmoor, Dead Sea, Deepwater, Delaware, Delhi, Denmark, Derwentwater, Detroit, Deptford, Dogger Bank, Don, Dover, Dresden, Dublin, Dulwich, Dumfries, Dunbar, Dunkirk,

Eddystone, Edmonton, Elba, Elgin, Ellis Island, Elsinore, Epping, Epsom, Essen, Ethonia, Estuary, Etheridge, Etna, Eton, Euston, Everest, Evesham, Falkland, Falmouth, Fashoda, Faversham, Felixstowe, Fernmouth, Fez, Fiji, Finisterre, Fishguard, Fiume, Flanders, Flinders, Flodden, Florence, Florida, Flushing, Ford, Forest, Formosa, Fort, Forth, Fotheringhay, Frankfort, Frogmore, Gallipoli, Galway, Ganges, Gaza, Geneva, Genoa, Georgia, Giant's Castle, Gibraltar, Glastonbury, Glamis, Glencoe, Golconda, Gold Coast, Good Hope, Goodleigh, Goodwin Sands, Goodwood, Goole, Goose Land, Gort, Granada, Grange, Gray's Inn, Grenoble, Great Belt, Great Wall, Greenland, Greenwich, Griffin, Guernsey, Gulora, Haddon Hall, Hague, Mail, Haiti, Hamburg,

Hampstead, Hanover, Harlech, Harris, Harwich, Hath, Hatton, Havana, Hawaii, Haymarket, Heligoland, Henley, Hereford, Heron, Hill Top, Hilltown, Hillswick, Hillside, Hodde, Hollywood, Holyrood, Honduras, Hong Kong, Holland, Hook of Holland, Honolulu, Horn, Hounslow, Hound-ditch, Hull, Humber, Hungary, Hush, Hyde Park, Iceland, Ilkley, Inkerman, Island Sea, Iona, Irishtown, Iron Gates, Italy, Ivanhoe, Jaffa, Jamaica, Japan, Java, Jericho, Johannesburg, John O' Groats, Jordan, Junction, Jutland, Kabul, Kale, Kandahar, Kansas, Kensington, Kentucky, Kenya, Keswick, Kew, Key West, Kiel, Kilkenny, Killiecrankie, Killarney, Kimberley, Kingstown, Kirkwall, Klondike, Knock, Kut,

Lapland, Lash, Lausanne, Leghorn, Lens, Lett, Letters, Letterewe, Lewis, Levant, Liffey, Light, Lille, Lima, Limerick, Lisbon, Little Belt, Little Britain, Lizard, Lochend, Loghill, Lombardy, Lomond, Loos, Lorraine, Lossiemouth, Lot, Lothian, Louvain, Lucknow, Luxor, Macedonia, Madeira, Madras, Madrid, Mafeking, Maine, Malacca, Malta, Malvern, Man, Manacles, Manwood, Marble Arch, March, Marines, Marmora, Marne, Maryland, Marylebone, Mayo, Medway, Menai Bridge, Menin, Melbourne, Melrose, Mentone, Mere, Mersey, Messina, Mexico, Michigan, Midland, Midtown, Milan, Mile End, Miles, Milford Haven, Millbank, Millwood, Minorca, Mint, Monaco, Mongolia, Mons, Monte Carlo, Monte Cristo, Montreal, Monument, Morocco, Mortlake, Moscow, Moss, Post,

Mount's Bay, Mull, Mudros, Nancy, Nanking, Naples, Naseby, Natal, Navarre, Naze, Needles, New Forest, New York, Newfoundland, Newgate, Newhaven, Newlands, Newmarket, Niagara, Nice, Niger, Nigeria, Nile, Nore, North Foreland, North Sea, Northcote, Norway, Nutley, Nutt, Nuttal, Oban, Odde, Odessa, Old, Oldbury, Olympia, Omdurman, Oran, Ontario, Oporto, Oregon, Orleans, Osborne, Osprey, Ostend, Ottawa, Oundle, Paddington, Padua, Pagoda, Palatine, Palm Beach, Panama, Papua, Park, Park Lane, Parkhill, Paris, Patagonia, Peak, Peking, Pentland, Peronne, Persia, Peru, Peshawar, Picardy, Pill, Piliar, Pisa, Plassey, Pompeii, Pontefract, Poplar, Port Arthur, Port Said, Portugal, Potsdam, Post,

Prague, Prestonpans, Pretoria, Providence, Punjab, Pyramid, Pyrenees, Quebec, Queensland, Queenstown, Quetta, Quito, Quorn, Raglan, Ramillies, Ramsay, Rangoon, Ravenswood, Recess, Red Castle, Reims, Reunion, Reval, Rhine, Rhineland, Rhodesia, Richborough, Richfield, Richmond, Ridout, Riff, Riga, River, Riviera, Riverside, Robe, Rockford, Rockwood, Roman, Rome, Rotterdam, Rosyth, Rouge, Round, Row, Runnymede, Ryde, Rye House, Sahara, Saintes, Sale, Samoa, Point San Reno, St. Helena, Salonica, Salt Lake, Sandhurst, Sandstone, Sandwich, Sarawak, Sardinia, Sark, Save, Savoy, Saxony, Scafell, Scapa Flow, Scutari, Seaforth, Seattle, Seaview, Sedan, Sedgmoor, Selkirk, Sert, Sevastopol, Seville, Shannon, Sheen, Shetland, Shiprock, Shoeburyness,

Siam, Siberia, Sicily, Silkstone, Silver City, Simla, Singapore, Skren, Skye, Slane, Sligo, Slite, Smyrna, Snowdon, Soda, Sofia, Soleut, Solway, Sombrero, Somme, Southwark, Spa, Spey, Spithead, Springfield, Springs, Stamboul, Stamford Bridge, Standon, Stanhope, Starcroes, Starlight, Stavanger, Steele, Sterling, Stepney, Stillman, Stockholm, Stonehenge, Stonewall, Stornoway, Strand, Stratford, Streator, Sudan, Suez, Summit, Sunbury, Suvla Bay, Swan, Swastika, Sydney, Tangier, Tank, Tasmania, Tay, Tees, Temple, Tennessee, Texas, Thebes, Three Hills, Three Rivers, Thunder Hill, Tibet, Tiber, Tiflis, Tigris, Timbertoo, Tipperary, Tivoli, Tobermory, Tokio, Toledo, Tongue, Toulon, Toulouse, Trafalgar, Transvaal, Trim, Trinidad, Tripoli, Trones Wood,

Trossachs, Troy, Tun, Tunis, Turin, Turkey, Tuscany, Tyrol, Tweed, Tweedale, Twelve Pins, Twin Hills, Tynehead, Ulster, Union, Utah, Valencia, Valenciennes, Valparaiso, Van, Vancouver, Venice, Verdun, Verona, Versailles, Vesuvius, Victoria, Vienna, Virginia, Viny, Volga, Vulcano, Wales, Walesby, Walkaway, Waltham, Warsaw, Wash, Washington, Waterdown, Waterloo, Watersmeet, Waverley, Wayne, Wear, Weed, Weedon, Welland, Wembley, West Acre, West Ham, Westminster, Westward Ho, Wexford, Whale, Whitebird, Whitehall, Windsor, Winnipeg, Woodcote, Woodland, Woodstock, Woolwich, Worms, Wrath, Wrekin, Wye, Wyoming, Yarmouth, Yellow Sea, Yellowstone, Yokohama, York, You, Youngstown, Ypres, Yukon, Zanzibar, Zeebrugge, Zuider Zee

£10 a Week for Life, or £4,000 Cash!

Second Prize, £300. Third Prize, £200.

THERE are prizes and prizes, but no popular journal has given you a prize to surpass this one. Consider—it is not an opportunity you can afford to turn down lightly!

You have only to solve eight puzzle-pictures a week for a few weeks, and there are no entrance fees or extras to pay. Here is the SECOND SET, each picture representing a name on the map—names all the world over, from Hyde Park to Hong Kong.

Don't worry whether you know your geography or not, because we give on the opposite page a Full List of Names from which every name denoted by a picture has been selected. For example: Picture No. 1 on this page clearly means MONTREAL.

For the benefit of new readers and any others who may have missed the opening puzzles, we have reprinted the First Set on this page. Those wishing to make more than one attempt to win our record prizes should also TAKE ADVANTAGE of this FREE GIFT.

Fill in your solution under each picture, and keep this set, together with the previous puzzles, until next week, when the Third Set will appear. The series consists of fifteen sets, and every effort must consist of the complete series.

The closing date is THURSDAY, MARCH 26th, 1925.

(FIRST SET REPRINTED.)

THE FIRST PRIZE of £4,000 (or £10 a week for life)

will be awarded to the reader who sends a correct, or most nearly correct solution of the fifteen sets of puzzle-pictures. The other prizes will be awarded in order of merit.

The Editor reserves full right to divide the prize-money as he thinks fit, should any ties make this necessary. No competitor will receive more than one prize.

It is a distinct condition of entry that the decision of the Editor be taken as final and legally binding throughout this contest, and entries will only be accepted on this understanding.

You may make as many different attempts as you please, but every attempt must be a complete solution of the whole series of puzzles; it must be quite distinct and separate from any other attempt. All solutions must be written IN INK, and entries mutilated or bearing alterations or alternative names will be disqualified.

No correspondence will be allowed. No responsibility can be taken for delay or loss in the post or otherwise. Proof of posting will not be accepted as proof of delivery.

This competition is run in conjunction with "Answers," "Pictorial Magazine," and "All Sports."

Employees of the proprietors of these journals may not compete.

DO NOT SEND IN ANY ENTRIES YET—WAIT UNTIL YOU HAVE ALL THE PUZZLES.